THE GECKO & STICKY
SINISTER SUBSTITUTE

Also by Wendelin Van Draanen

The Gecko and Sticky: Villain's Lair

The Gecko and Sticky: The Greatest Power

Shredderman: Secret Identity

Shredderman: Attack of the Tagger

Shredderman: Meet the Gecko

Shredderman: Enemy Spy

Sammy Keyes and the Hotel Thief

Sammy Keyes and the Skeleton Man

Sammy Keyes and the Sisters of Mercy

Sammy Keyes and the Runaway Elf

Sammy Keyes and the Curse of Moustache Mary

Sammy Keyes and the Hollywood Mummy

Sammy Keyes and the Search for Snake Eyes

Sammy Keyes and the Art of Deception

Sammy Keyes and the Psycho Kitty Queen

Sammy Keyes and the Dead Giveaway

Sammy Keyes and the Wild Things

Sammy Keyes and the Cold Hard Cash

WENDELIN VAN DRAANEN

THE GECKO & STICKY
SINISTER SUBSTITUTE

ILLUSTRATED BY
STEPHEN GILPIN

ALFRED A. KNOPF · NEW YORK

THIS IS A BORZOI BOOK PUBLISHED BY ALFRED A. KNOPF

Visit us on the Web! www.randomhouse.com/kids

Educators and librarians, for a variety of teaching tools, visit us at
www.randomhouse.com/teachers

Library of Congress Cataloging-in-Publication Data
Van Draanen, Wendelin.
The Gecko and Sticky : sinister substitute / by Wendelin Van Draanen ; illustrations by Stephen Gilpin. — 1st ed.
p. cm. — (The Gecko and Sticky)
Summary: Seventh-grader Dave Sanchez and his talking gecko sidekick Sticky decide they must rescue an odious science teacher who has been kidnapped by the even more villainous Damien Black, who is masquerading as a substitute teacher in order to steal Dave's magic Aztec wristband.
ISBN 978-0-375-84378-5 (trade) — ISBN 978-0-375-94572-4 (lib. bdg.) —
ISBN 978-0-375-89492-3 (e-book)
[1. Adventure and adventurers—Fiction. 2. Substitute teachers—Fiction. 3. Magic—Fiction. 4. Schools—Fiction. 5. Geckos—Fiction. 6. Lizards—Fiction. 7. Hispanic Americans—Fiction.] 1. Gilpin, Stephen, ill. II. Title. III. Title: Sinister substitute.
PZ7.V2745Gc2010
[Fic]—dc22
2009014888

Printed in the United States of America
January 2010
10 9 8 7 6 5 4 3 2 1

First Edition

Dedicated to children's book wizard Tim Wadham,
whose support helped bring the Gecko and Sticky to life.

CONTENTS

Chapter 1
A DOOZY OF A DAY

The day did not start well for Dave Sanchez.

First, his alarm didn't go off.

Then his little sister, Evie, stubbornly stayed locked inside the bathroom (because she knew that Dave really, really, really needed to use it).

This was followed by several mishaps (including a frantic search for gym shorts, a stubbed toe, and a broken plate of scrambled eggs).

And (as if he wasn't running late enough already) his gecko lizard decided at the last minute to stay home.

"Come *on*, Sticky!" Dave whispered into the crack behind his bookshelf.

"I don't think so, *señor*," the gecko replied.

"That scary *señorita* is making you slice and dice frogs today, remember?"

Allow me to pause here a moment to clarify something:

Yes, the gecko talks.

Let me also make clear right off the bat that this is not some silly story where make-believe animals act all cutesy-wootsy and talk to each other.

No, this story is quite true.

This gecko is quite *real*.

And don't worry—I won't be springing talking cats or dogs or cows or burros (or monkeys, for that matter) on you. The gecko and *only* the gecko talks, and that's because . . .

Well, nobody's really sure. Some people believe Sticky is bewitched or cursed or possessed or a shape-shifting evil entity who's plotting to ruin lives, but people are often fearful of things they can't explain. So let's get on with Dave's manic

morning, shall we? It is, after all, in the middle of going from bad to worse.

"You're still here?" his mother gasped when she saw Dave crouched beside his bookcase. "You're going to be late for school!"

"I know, Mom!" Dave snapped, and since the fact that Sticky could talk was top-secret (because Sticky had vowed to never speak again if Dave spilled the beans to anyone), he simply gave up on the lizard, grabbed his backpack and bike, and left for school.

Unfortunately, his neighbor Lily was also running late for school, and she was in no mood to follow Dave and his dorky bike down seven flights of stairs.

"Out of my way, delivery boy!" she said, trying to squeeze past him.

So Dave (who had his bike hoisted onto his shoulder) swung to the left at the next landing in an effort to get out of her way. But Lily had been

trying to squeeze past him on the right (a no-no maneuver in any traffic situation, be it highway or stairway) and got smacked against the shoulder by the rear tire.

"Ow!" she cried as she stumbled into the wall.

Dave apologized, but Lily Espinoza was not the sort of girl who accepted apologies from dorky boys who hoisted their bikes up and down stairs. And after she was done using language that made Dave want to retreat like a turtle inside his bike helmet, she stormed past him and charged off to school.

It was, I'm sure you'll agree, a doozy of a day already, but then a new wave of misfortune began:

As fate would have it, Dave got a flat tire and had to lock his bike to a streetlight and run the last three blocks to school. He was, of course, late. And late at Geronimo Middle School meant lunchtime detention.

"Here you go, Mr. Sanchez," the attendance

secretary said, handing Dave a slip that would allow him to get into his first-period class.

"Thanks," Dave sighed, and shuffled off to pre-algebra, where, to his dismay, he couldn't find his homework. Unfortunately, his teacher, Mr. Vye, did not believe in late homework. He believed in zeroes and detentions and parent conferences, but late homework? Oh no.

In his next class, he *could* find his homework, but he'd done the wrong questions. (Right numbers, wrong page.) Ms. DeWitt was sympathetic, but her allowing him to make up the assignment (and, consequently, doubling the social studies homework that night) was almost worse than receiving a zero.

Then, in language, Dave sat in his seat and discovered there was some sort of puddle on it. (He didn't want to know or imagine what.) His backside now looked sadly soggy, and, of course, this was the day Ms. Huff called on him to go to the board and conjugate the verb "to lie" (by which, unfortunately, she did not mean the "to lie" that means "to tell an untruth," but rather the one that means "to lie down").

Dave had never been so glad to get to P.E. and switch out of his clothes, only someone had broken into his locker and stolen his shirt. (His shorts, you may recall, were with him, as he'd had his mother repair an embarrassing rip in the inseam.)

"Oh great," he grumbled, and trudged over to Mr. Wilson's office to get a loaner.

"Last loaner for this quarter, Mr. Sanchez. Next time, your grade drops."

"But someone broke into my locker!"

"Uh-huh," his teacher replied, and without question this "Uh-huh" meant "Yeah, *right*."

"It's true!" Dave countered. "People get stuff stolen from their lockers all the time—can't you do something about it?"

"Uh-huh," Mr. Wilson said again. "I can get you to click your lock closed, and if you don't, I can give you a loaner and dock your grade."

"But I *did* close my lock."

"Uh-huh."

Now, I could tell you the rest of the conversation, but why subject you to it? Obviously, Mr. Wilson didn't believe Dave. Obviously, Dave was upset (and, I might add, rightly so).

So after P.E. had ended and Dave had collected two shin bruises for his efforts in soccer, he was (as I'm sure you can imagine) in one bad mood. And he was trudging off to the cafeteria to serve his lunchtime detention (looking every bit as grumpy and glum as he felt) when he bumped into Lily Espinoza.

Again.

This time, however, there was no bike involved. This time she was bubbling with excitement. "Did you hear?" she asked Dave.

Dave was a little stunned, as Lily wasn't treating him at all like he was her dorky, dangerously klutzy neighbor. She seemed actually happy to see him.

"Uh . . . hear what?" Dave asked.

"The Crocodile is absent!"

"Ms. Krockle is?" Dave pumped a fist. "Yes!"

To his continued surprise, Lily pumped her fist, too, then moved on to further spread the giddifying news.

Well! What, you may ask, could this Ms. Krockle be like to evoke such a response from both Lily and Dave (and, in truth, from each and every member of the seventh-grade class)?

Let me attempt to explain:

Ms. Veronica Krockle is severe.

Strict.

And worse than both those combined, sarcastic.

"Another stellar performance," she would tell a failing student. "The studying must have been exhausting. Really, do take some time off to recuperate."

She had sarcasm down to a science.

But not only was she painful to be around, she was painful to look at.

Imagine a woman with too many teeth, too little hair, a snarl for a mouth, and pointy yellow fingernails. Then put that woman in a knee-length lab coat and high-heeled black boots, and you have a pretty fair picture of Ms. Veronica Krockle.

Ms. Veronica Krockle, who, I might add, relished the slicey-dicey dissection of frogs.

Yes, of all the fizzy-foamy,

smoky-choky labs her students did in science, dissecting frogs was the one she really looked forward to. For weeks before the scalpels came out she would chortle and snort in anticipation. Fainting girls, green-gilled boys, queasy, squealing students . . . Ms. Veronica Krockle would not miss it for the world.

And yet . . .

And yet on this particular frog-slicing day she was absent.

It was, in fact, her first absence in the nine years she'd been teaching at Geronimo Middle School. Never had phlegmy colds or fiery fevers or scratchy rashes or sties in the eyes or great gusting bouts of gas kept her away.

She was there, without fail, each and every day.

So this was, truly, a rare and joyous occasion.

But it was also strange.

Ah, yes. As Dave would soon discover, it was very strange indeed.

Chapter 2
THE SUBSTITUTE

It's a well-known fact among people in education that substitute teachers are saints. You may not be aware of this well-known fact, but that's most likely because you're on the receiving end of a substitute's mission to maintain law and order (and, if time allows and they know the material, teach a little).

It's also a well-known fact (this time among students) that substitute teachers are either too lax or too strict; either you're allowed to monkey around or you're barely allowed to breathe.

Both kinds are, for the record, still saints because no matter when they're called in to work, it's always feeding time at the zoo.

Now, by "feeding time at the zoo," I do not mean the feeding of hungry young minds.

Oh no.

By "feeding time at the zoo," I mean the tossing of a single well-intentioned adult into a cage of thirty or more monkeys hungry for a little fun. And the students in Ms. Krockle's class were, without question, ravenous. To them, this day was like uncovering a Reese's peanut butter cup on a plate of broccoli.

Like discovering chocolate milk in a bottle of V8.

Like finding Cap'n Crunch in a box of All-Bran!

In a word, sw-eeeet!

It was almost irrelevant whether the substitute was a lax one or a strict one. Even the strictest of substitutes would be a pushover compared to the ironfisted Veronica Krockle.

It was a popular boy named Fons Soto who

started the fun. "Switch seats!" he whispered to the kids around him as they filed into fifth period. "Everybody!"

And so it was that Dave wound up in Reuben Medina's seat, Reuben Medina wound up in Fons Soto's seat, and Fons wound up in Dave's seat.

The rest of the class, too, was completely scrambled.

"Good afternoon," the substitute said. "My name is Dr. Schwarz, and I have the distinct pleasure of delving into the fascinating complexities of science with you today."

Having been so intensely absorbed in the switching of seats, the students had, until now, avoided looking at the substitute. But now that they *were* looking, each and every jaw dropped.

Dr. Schwarz looked like something out of a storybook: Dressed in a tweed suit (complete with matching vest), he wore stylish rectangular horn-rimmed glasses and held a pipe. (Yes, the sort that's smoked, as opposed to the sort you might run water through or, say, clonk against a villain's head.)

He had a full head of dark hair, with just a smattering of gray (giving him a distinguished, professorial look), and a gold watch on a chain was tucked neatly inside a waistcoat pocket.

"So!" he said, chomping down on his pipe (which, due to smoking regulations, was not lit). "What do you want to talk about?"

Thirty pairs of eyes went this way and that, signaling, "Is he serious?" in the sly and semaphore-ish manner only teenage eyes can.

And when the signals that returned were "I think so!" thirty minds kicked into immediate overdrive, thinking, Oh, this guy's gonna be *easy* to mess with.

Dr. Schwarz laughed. "Surely you don't want to dissect frogs. . . ."

"I do!" a boy named Greg Lazo (who was, incidentally, sitting in Tyler Mills's seat) called from the back of the class.

All the students whipped around in their seats to shoot Greg down with their semaphore-ish eyes.

"Well, I *do*," he said meekly.

Dr. Schwarz went to the podium and scanned the seating chart. "Well, Tyler," he said, looking directly at Greg, "let's rethink your position on this, shall we? Because frogs are one of nature's most magnificent creatures. Why, did you know that most frogs can jump twenty times their own body length? That would be like you jumping one hundred feet! Could you imagine?" He paused for Greg (or, according to the seating chart, Tyler) to imagine himself hopping such a distance, then quietly asked, "Why would we want to kill and dissect such a wonder?"

"But they're already dead," Greg muttered.

The rest of the class whipped around again.

"But they are!" Greg grumbled.

"Ah, young man," Dr. Schwarz said with a gentle tisk. "You have so much to learn." He gave Greg a wink. "Which, I suppose, is why you're in school, hmm?"

Dr. Schwarz was now pacing, his hands and his pipe clasped behind his back. "Perhaps you'd be more sympathetic if the subject were a snake?" He looked around the room. "How many of you like snakes?"

All the boys (including Greg Lazo) raised their hands.

All the girls (especially Lily Espinoza) left theirs firmly in their laps.

"How about . . . iguanas? Hmm?"

This time, almost all hands went up.

"How many of you *own* an iguana?"

To everyone's surprise, Yasmine Branson (who was known for her addiction to peanut M&M's and little else) said, "I do."

Dr. Schwarz consulted the seating chart, gave Yasmine a warm smile, and said, "Amazing, aren't they, Carla?"

Yasmine smiled uncomfortably as her head bobbed up and down.

It's fair to say that at this point the students were beginning to regret their little seating prank. Tyler Mills, especially, did not like Dr. Schwarz thinking he was the one who wanted to kill and dissect frogs. But what else could they do but play along?

"What about chameleons?" Dr. Schwarz asked, pacing thoughtfully as he looked around the room. "Don't you wish you could change colors like they do? Wouldn't it be fun to camouflage yourself that way?" He dropped his voice in a conspiratorial manner. "Imagine if you were walking the halls without a pass and the principal was coming and you could instantly take on the shade and markings of the wall!" He chuckled. "Wouldn't that be fantastic?"

And that was it. With the possible exception of Greg Lazo, every student in Ms. Veronica Krockle's fifth-period class instantly liked their substitute.

He wasn't just a spiffy dresser.

He wasn't just nixing the dissection of frogs.

He was funny!

Understanding!

In a word, *cool*.

But then came a question that gave one particular student pause:

"How about geckos?" Dr. Schwarz asked. "Know anybody with a pet gecko?"

The particular student pausing was, as you've almost certainly guessed, Dave Sanchez. Since Sticky had moved into Dave's apartment, Dave had taken him to school almost every day because, well, Sticky was his little buddy.

However, bringing pets to school was against the rules, and since there was the additional worry over Sticky being no ordinary gecko, the lizard spent most of the school day snoozing inside Dave's backpack or quietly cruising the campus for bugs and some sizzly sunshine. So (amazingly enough) it was not common knowledge that Dave had a pet gecko, which is the way Sticky liked it. "If someone sees me, *señor*," he had instructed Dave, "just tell them you found me outside."

This was, I might add, a perfectly reasonable thing to say, given the nature of nature in the area. Geckos were common. Found here and there in gardens or buildings or just stuck to walls soaking in the afternoon sun.

And since it's a long-held belief that geckos bring luck, nobody minded finding one hanging from the ceiling of their sitting room.

Or bathroom.

Or classroom.

So although someone asking about geckos was, to the average student, no big deal, to Dave it was.

Especially since his gecko was no ordinary gecko.

And double-especially since it wasn't just *having* a gecko that was supposed to stay secret. There was another secret much bigger than that.

A life-and-death get-caught-and-you're-toast sort of secret.

And it was most definitely connected to geckos.

Chapter 3
BIZARRE AND BAMBOOZLING

We are now at the part of the story where I ask myself, How in the world am I going to explain this and not have you say, "Yeah, *right.*"

I will do my best, and all I ask is that you don't jump in and say, "Yeah, *right,*" right away.

All right?

All right. Here goes:

When Sticky moved into Dave's apartment, he brought with him an ancient Aztec wristband. A *magic* Aztec wristband also known as a power-band. One that, when matched with special notched ingots, could make the wearer invisible.

Or super-strong.

Or lightning fast.

And for the first time since he learned of the unexpected absence of Ms. Veronica Krockle, the situation seemed to Dave to be a bit odd.

Almost creepy.

Who was this man?

He sure wasn't *teaching* them anything.

Maybe he wasn't a teacher at all!

Maybe he was a reporter!

Someone who was trying to find out who the Gecko was!

But . . . why was he at Geronimo Middle School?

Why not some other school?

Why not just out on the street looking for curiously compact men?

Had somebody tipped him off?

But . . . they wouldn't let some reporter teach science!

That was crazy!

Still, what had happened to Ms. Krockle? Her

absence on an ordinary day would have been un-usual enough, but being gone on dissection day? There was something strange about this.

Something peculiar and suspicious.

In a word, fishy.

Especially since Dr. Schwarz didn't move along to the subject of some other radical reptile. He stayed on the subject of geckos.

"What?" he asked the silent class. "Don't *any* of you know someone with a pet gecko?"

Now, it is a well-known fact that middle-school children do not yet have the wisdom of adults. (Well, it's a well-known fact among adults, anyway.)

What middle-school children *do* have, how-ever, is a keen sense of manipulation. Not only are they experts in manipulating others, but they are also able to recognize when someone is manipu-lating them.

This is why the vibe in Ms. Krockle's science room began to change.

Seventh-grade sonar went up.

Manipulation radar kicked in.

And as new vibes moved quickly from student to student, Dr. Schwarz stood there, oblivious. "How about extra credit," he said, a testy edge creeping into his voice. "Extra credit for anyone with a gecko, or anyone who knows anyone with a gecko."

It was at this point that Dave felt Lily Espinoza staring at him, and with a surge of panic, he turned to face her.

Lily knew he had a gecko!

(Or, at least, she'd seen him rescue Sticky from her cat a bunch of times.)

And Lily could really use some extra credit in science!

(And, for that matter, every other course she was taking.)

And although Dave was aware that Lily Espinoza thought he was a klutzy, dorky "delivery boy" who liked to knock her flat with his bike, he still needed to at least *try* to keep her quiet. So, with his eyes locked on hers, Dave slyly lifted a finger to his lips and wobbled his head ever so slightly.

Lily raised one eyebrow, frowned, and looked away.

Meanwhile, Fons Soto (who, you may recall, was sitting in Dave Sanchez's seat) decided to have a little fun. "Hey, *Calvin*," he called, looking across the classroom at Ricky Zaragoza. "Where's your gecko, man?"

"Me?" Ricky asked, pointing to himself (because he was, indeed, sitting in Calvin Jones's seat). "Uh, I don't have a gecko." He hesitated, then looked over at Dave. "But I think, uh, *Reuben* might."

Dave felt little beads of sweat pop from his forehead, but he acted as cool as possible. "Nah," Dave said. Then he passed along the gecko baton. "But, *Fons*, don't you have one?"

"Me?" Reuben Medina said, pointing to himself. "No way. But hey, *Tyler*," he called toward Greg Lazo, "don't you have one?"

It was, indeed, a big jumble of names and remembering who was sitting in whose seat.

Then Greg said, "Look, if I go outside and catch one, can I get extra credit?"

Dr. Schwarz frowned. "No."

"Okaaaay . . . ," Greg said. "How about I catch one anyway, and we dissect it?"

"Eeeew!" all the girls squealed.

"No way!" all the boys snapped.

Dr. Schwarz, however, didn't utter a sound. Instead, his frown deepened and his eyes narrowed as he peered at the students suspiciously.

This, of course, caused Dave to shrink into his seat and shudder. And if he'd had lingering doubts before, they were now gone.

There was definitely something strange about this substitute.

Chapter 4
THE HAZARDS OF PRANKING THE SUBSTITUTE

Dave had never been so glad to get away from Ms. Krockle's classroom. (Which is, as you know, really saying something.)

He had also never been so spaced out during drama. He sat through this last class of the day blurry-brained with worry. Was Dr. Schwarz a reporter?

An investigator?

Why was he so interested in geckos?

Did he know the Gecko *had* a gecko?

How would he know that?

What did this all mean?

Dave was still spaced out when school let out. So much so that he circled the bike racks again and again before he remembered that his bike was chained to a streetlight three blocks from school, looking forlorn and forsaken with its flabby flat tire.

Now, had this disastrous day continued in the same vein (or if I were, say, just making this up), Dave would have returned to the streetlight to discover that his bike had been stolen, and (hmm, let's see) then a mugger would have pounced from a nearby convenience store, stripping him of his wallet (and, oh, maybe his *shoes*), and Dave would have had to walk the rest of the way home barefoot and broke (facing off with a pit bull or two along the way).

But (fortunately for Dave) I'm *not* making this up. The fact is, Dave returned to his bike, fixed the flat, and set about making up for lost time. Dave, you see, was called "delivery boy" by Lily for a reason. He couriered packages and envelopes between businesses in the downtown area, and besides building up a tidy sum of money for his efforts, he had also built up a reputation for punctuality, neatness, and speed.

On this particular afternoon, however, Dave's hard-earned reputation was in danger as he was late, smudged, and (quite frankly) beat.

But Dave made his rounds with as much professionalism as he could muster and managed to drag himself (and his bike) up the stairs to his apartment before his parents and Evie returned home.

Dave would have liked nothing more than to simply collapse on his bed and forget about his horrible day, but he couldn't.

He was still worried.

"Sticky?" he whispered, peering behind his bookcase, but Sticky was not there.

"Sticky?" he said more loudly, looking around his room, but Sticky did not appear.

"Sticky!" he called, wandering through the

apartment, at last venturing over to the kitchen window and lifting it fully open.

"Hey, *hombre*," came a stretchy, sleepy voice from the flower box outside. "What took you so long?"

So Dave lifted his little buddy inside and told him about Dr. Schwarz and his keen interest in geckos.

"Are you serious, man?" Sticky asked.

"Of course I'm serious! I've been freaked out about it all day. I think he's a reporter. Or some guy from the FBI or something."

"Hmm," Sticky said (in a maddeningly calm manner). He cocked his little gecko head.

He tapped his little gecko chin.

He hmm'd again.

And at last he said, "Do you think he'll be there tomorrow? I could check him out, *señor*."

"Tomorrow? No! Krockle's not going to miss *two* days. It's a miracle she missed one!"

But Ms. Veronica Krockle was, indeed, absent the next day.

And Dr. Schwarz was again her substitute.

"Uh-oh," Fons Soto said when he saw Dr. Schwarz through the open doorway. "Same seats as yesterday," he whispered to the kids around him. "And don't get busted!"

So once again Fons sat in Dave's seat, Dave sat in Reuben's seat, Reuben sat in Fons's seat, and so on and so forth. And when they were all seated, Dr. Schwarz smiled across the expanse of somewhat guilty faces and said, "So! Who brought in extra credit?"

Tyler Mills had, in fact, brought in a gecko. He had spent his lunchtime searching, and had finally captured a very handsome banded gecko.

Unfortunately for Tyler, he was in a terribly uncomfortable position. Raising his hand and saying, "I have a gecko!" would result in Eli Laslow getting the extra credit (as that's whose seat Tyler was in). Yet explaining who he really was would result in his ratting out the rest of the class.

Ah, the hazards of pranking the substitute.

To circumvent the problem, Tyler slipped the gecko to Greg Lazo (as Greg was, once again, sitting in Tyler's seat) with the understanding that Greg would continue the seating charade by raising his hand and saying, "I have a gecko!"

Unfortunately for Tyler, Greg had seized upon this as an opportunity for blackmail. "It'll cost ya five bucks," he whispered.

The whole situation had become one big jumbled shouldn't-have-pranked-the-substitute mess, but what could Tyler do?

He slipped Greg a five.

Now, Greg did hold up his end of the bargain, but for all the interest Dr. Schwarz had professed to have in geckos, he paid the one Greg held very little attention. "That's it?" he

asked after giving the banded gecko a quick inspection. "No one else has one?"

No one volunteered, but someone else did (as you know) have one.

One that was staying uncharacteristically quiet.

One that had been watching the professor's every move from a sneaky-peeky spy spot inside Dave's sweatshirt.

One that had been thinking how this strange man in the tweed suit and horn-rimmed glasses was strangely familiar.

(Dr. Schwarz was, in fact, wearing the exact same outfit he had worn the day before, something that further raised the growing *ewww* factor in the eyes of the girls.)

And then Dr. Schwarz moved slowly, purposefully toward Dave's assigned seat, where he stopped.

He gazed down at Fons Soto and raised one

dark eyebrow. "I've been told that *you* have a gecko, Mr. Sanchez. Why didn't you bring him in?"

And then Dr. Schwarz made a fateful mistake.

He smiled.

"Hopping *habañeros!*" Sticky gasped (ever so quietly) from his sneaky-peeky spy spot. "That's no teacher! That's Damien Black!"

Chapter 5
THE DEADLY, DIABOLICAL DAMIEN BLACK

Ah, yes.

Damien Black.

Is there a more diabolical villain on the face of the earth?

I think not.

Besides being a ruthless treasure hunter, Damien Black is many things:

For one, he is a builder. His mansion (which looms large and lonely atop an area of the city known as Raven Ridge) was once simply a spooky old house with the classic dangling shutters and pointy spires and slipping shingles (and, of course, owls that went *whooo* in the night).

It is still that, but it is now much more.

Damien, you see, added mysterious rooms (which jut out at odd angles), secret passages (which go to sinister places), strange elevators (which can be quite deadly), and confounding corridors (which lead everywhere or nowhere, depending on when you turn).

Beneath the mansion, Damien has done extensive and expansive (and, without a doubt, *expensive*) excavation. There's an entire city of caves and cages and cavernous closets (not to mention a gilded coffee café, which, until recently, was tended by a java-junkie monkey, but that's another story).

Damien Black is also an inventor. From wacky walkie-talkies to spiffy Sewer Cruisers to funky-doodle infrared glasses, Damien Black is a fiend for kooky (and complicated) contraptions. And since he always seems to have a need for things you just can't buy, Damien builds his own thinga-majigs and thingamabobs, and cobbles together death-dealing doohickeys, villainous whatsits, and widgety-gadgety gizmos.

Over time he has amassed an enormous arsenal of wicked, tricky toys.

Damien Black is *also* . . . Well, really, you don't want me to list them all, now do you? I could go on and on about him being (among other things) a stealth pilot and a dragon trainer and a man who despises children, but let's just fast-forward to the particular thing that matters at this particular point, shall we?

And that particular thing is: disguise artist.

Damien Black is, without question, the Master of Disguise.

Hmm. It occurs to me that since I mentioned *dragons* before, you may be thinking that by "Master of Disguise," I mean a shape-shifter.

I do not.

I *would* not.

This is, after all, a *true* story, not one that

resorts to fabricated powers and spells and people who can willy-nilly their way through difficult circumstances by miraculously changing their shape.

Please.

Everyone knows there's no such thing as a shape-shifter.

And yes, I did refer to a dragon before, but I was talking about Damien's *Komodo* dragon (not some mythological beast found in stories with willy-nilly shape-shifters).

No, when I say that Damien Black is the Master of Disguise, I mean that the man knows how to masquerade as people (and, for that matter, *things*) that in no way resemble his dastardly, devilish self.

This talent does not come easy.

Or cheap.

He has an enormous underground cavern-like closet that holds (aside from several well-positioned cheval mirrors) all manner of disguises.

This was no teacher!

This was the deadly, diabolical Damien Black!

Now, if there's one thing Damien loves to twist (besides the truth), it's his long, sinister mustache. It's like a good-luck charm.

A twin-tailed talisman.

A hairy amulet.

(Or, if you will, a soft and soothing security blanket for his tight upper lip.)

So what would possess him to shave it off?

Well, aside from the comforting thought that it would, indeed, grow back, Damien was willing to sacrifice the mustache to get something he really, really wanted:

Dave's powerband.

Which had, at one point, been *his* powerband.

To make a very long story short, Damien (at this point in time) still possessed every ingot that went with the powerband save one:

Wall-Walker.

Dave, on the other hand, had only Wall-Walker, but he did, in fact, possess the one and only powerband.

Having owned it (and Sticky) at one point, Damien was desperate to get his maniacal mitts back on the powerband (and maybe Sticky, too, so he could get rid of that yakkity-yakking trouble-making lizard once and for all). So, as run-ins with Dave (as the Gecko) occurred, Damien slowly gathered clues about Dave's identity.

He did not know Dave's name or where he lived, but the last time they'd clashed, Damien had seen an eagle insignia on the boy's T-shirt.

An eagle insignia that had GMS underneath it.

It did not take a diabolically devilish brain to decode this, but (as demented villains are prone) Damien felt extremely clever when he'd worked out its meaning.

"Bwaa-ha-ha-ha-ha!" he'd laughed. "Geronimo

Middle School! 'Home of the Eagles'! Bwaa-ha-ha-ha-ha!"

And so he had paced and pondered and plotted. And after countless hours of fine-tuning and finessing, he had, at long last, hatched a plan.

A plan that was now in full sinister swing in Ms. Veronica Krockle's science classroom.

As Damien towered above Fons Soto (or, according to his seating chart, Dave Sanchez) and confronted him about owning a gecko, he knew he was close to getting what he wanted.

He could just *feel* it.

This boy was definitely hiding something.

And the whole class was obviously helping him!

The air was positively charged with lies!

Sneaky, snotty, bratty-faced lies!

"Uh, not me," Fons said with a nervous laugh. "Actually, I've *never* owned a gecko." Then he added, "Maybe someone's just messin' with your head?"

Messing, indeed!

Unfortunately for Damien Black, he misinterpreted just *how* these students were messing with his head, and as he sneered at Fons Soto, his dark, deadly eyes danced with laughter.

This Dave Sanchez boy was no match for him!

After school, he would follow him.

Corner him!

Once again the powerband would be his!

Bwaa-ha-ha-ha-ha!

Chapter 6
AFTER SCHOOL

After school, Damien Black did, indeed, follow Fons Soto (who he thought was named Dave Sanchez).

And Dave and Sticky followed Damien Black.

Dave had slipped into his own (not-so-elaborate) disguise: black shirt, dark shades, ball cap. He'd also clicked in the Wall-Walker ingot and was making full use of his ability to move quickly along roofline shadows, unnoticed.

Damien, on the other hand, had done a speedy job of disguising his disguise by dumping the glasses, pocket watch, pipe, coat, and vest. Instead of an eccentric professor, he now looked like a tall, lanky, narrow-nosed nerd.

"Are you *sure* that's Damien Black?" Dave whispered to Sticky. "It doesn't look anything like him!"

"Ay-ay-ay," Sticky grumbled. "Trust me for once, would you, *señor?*" He cocked his head at Dave. "Why else would he be following that boy?"

"Maybe they're just going the same direction?"

Sticky rolled his eyes. "Don't be a *bobo* dingo. It's him."

"Okay, so if it *is* him," Dave said after shadowing the sinister substitute for another minute, "what are we going to do?"

"Hmm," Sticky said, tapping his little gecko chin as he and Dave moved along a good twenty feet above Damien. "You really want my advice, *señor?*"

"Uh, yeah," Dave said (in a drawn-out, all-knowing-thirteen-year-old way).

Sticky eyed him. "And you'll *take* my advice this time?"

"I always take your advice."

"No, *señor*, you don't."

"Yes, I do!"

"No, you don't!"

"Yes, I do!"

Sticky thought for a moment, then shook his head. "Never mind. Just do whatever you want."

"But I don't know what I want to do!"

"So you'll take my advice?"

"Sticky! Just tell me!"

"Okay, *señor*. I think you should do this." And before Dave knew what was happening, Sticky was up on his hind legs with his hands cupped around his mouth, shouting, "HEY, DONKEY BREATH!" down at Damien.

Dave froze. "What are you *doing*?" he said through gritted teeth, but it was too late.

Damien looked up.

"YEAH, YOU!" Sticky shouted down at

Damien (although Sticky's amazingly loud voice sounded for all the world like it was coming from Dave). "YOU THINK I DON'T KNOW WHO YOU ARE, YOU BLACK-HEARTED BOZO?" Then Sticky dropped his voice and said to Dave, "There you go, *señor*. Our work here is done."

Sticky, of course, was quite right. Why would Damien follow Fons Soto when "Dave Sanchez" was obviously not the one with the powerband? "Dave Sanchez" couldn't possibly be the Gecko.

The real Dave, however, was having a little trouble processing this. And so (as is usually the case when one is stunned, shocked, or just plain mentally zapped) Dave stayed there, frozen (in this case to the wall).

Damien, too, was shocked, and although the rest of him stayed put, his jaw dropped.

His eyes caught fire.

His mind spattered and sputtered until sparks seemed to fly from his dastardly ears.

"*Ándale, hombre!*" Sticky whispered to Dave. "Unless you still don't believe me . . . ?"

So, lickety-split, Dave scurried over the roof and out of Damien's view, but he was not happy. Not happy at all. "I can't believe you did that!" he said to Sticky. "That was crazy! What if he comes after us?"

"Ay-ay-ay," Sticky grumbled. "This is the thanks I get for sizzly-quick thinking?"

"Sticky! It was crazy!"

Sticky shrugged. "But it worked, right?"

Dave had to admit that yes, it had worked. And after he got over the shock of Sticky's brash tactic, he had one big worry remaining. "What if he's back tomorrow?"

"Hmm," Sticky said, the wheels in his brain clickity-clacking like crazy. At last, he asked, "Uh . . . you say that scary *señorita* has never missed a day? Ever?"

"That's what I've heard. And she's been there *for*

"*Sí, señor.*" Sticky took another deep breath and then blurted, "I think that *loco* honcho has her."

Dave nearly collided with a car as the significance of Sticky's words sank in. He swerved to the curb, then stopped and stared at the gecko. "You think Damien Black *kidnapped* her?"

Sticky's head bobbed solemnly. "If I know that evil *hombre*, he's got her locked up inside that crazy *casa*. And, *señor*, there's only one way to stop him from coming back to school." He looked directly at Dave. "You have to rescue her."

Chapter 7
SIMMERING SOUP

Damien Black did not live alone in his maniacal mansion on Raven Ridge.

Oh, he would have *liked* to, but three men (who were known in their hometown as the Bandito Brothers) had, at one point, bumbled their way into his house, and try as he might to get rid of them, they always seemed to come back.

The Bandito Brothers—Tito, Angelo, and Pablo—were not actual brothers (although they fought like they were). They were a mariachi band.

A *bad* one.

They screeched out songs.

Played out of tune.

And (as it was their real purpose in forming the band) they stole stuff.

Yes, the Bandito Brothers played at being a band, but they were actually a band of thieves. And in all their crooked years, these out-of-tune crooners had never met another thief, another swindler, another *anyone* as clever as Damien Black.

They were, it's fair to say, awestruck by the treasure hunter. And, despite the fact that Damien called them bumbling bozos and had, on several occasions, come close to killing them, the Brothers were sure that deep in his dark, dastardly heart, Damien Black liked them.

And so, time after time, the Bandito Brothers returned to the monstrous mansion from which they'd been banned, in hopes that someday they, too, would be clever and crafty and rich like Damien Black.

Now, the simple truth is, Sticky was right:

Damien had, indeed, abducted Ms. Veronica Krockle.

And Damien had (to his sinister surprise) discovered that he couldn't handle her alone.

Oh, he'd had no problem clonking her over the head (with the smooth, appropriately twisted, and remarkably dense humerus of a pygmy hippo—a bone he'd acquired while on a hippo safari in the forests of Tiwai Island).

He'd had no problem blindfolding her and transporting her up to Raven Ridge (in his devilishly dandy 1959 Cadillac Eldorado).

And he'd had no problem hoisting her like a rag doll up ninety-nine steps to a remote, windowless tower in his maze of a mansion and locking her up.

But after she came to?

Oh my.

Damien discovered (to his horror) that he'd abducted a mad cat.

An angry alligator!

A wild and wicked wasp of a woman!

And what a stinger that voice of hers was!

And so, once again, he'd turned to the Bandito Brothers for help.

"Tie her up and *shut* her up!" he'd commanded.

"Who *is* she?" they'd asked.

"Just do it!" he'd snapped, and shoved them inside the tower room with a fat roll of duct tape.

Damien was not, I should point out, a coward. He simply did not want Veronica Krockle to see him, or to know where she had been taken (hence the windowlessness of the room). His plan was neither to keep her nor to kill her. Oh no. She was not nearly important enough for *that*. He just needed her out of the way until he'd tracked down the boy and snatched back the powerband.

His plan was to then return Ms. Veronica Krockle to Geronimo Middle School (late at night and blindfolded, of course) and be done with the whole maddening mess without *making* a mess (by, say, killing her).

But, Damien now thought as he zoomed home and changed out of his disguise, this was all taking longer than he'd expected.

Way longer.

And since (as we all know) desperate, diabolical times call for desperate, diabolical measures, he began plotting ways to adjust his plan.

He had to figure out what to do next!

And when, exactly, to rid himself of that nasty cat-scratch teacher.

Apparently he wasn't the only one thinking this, as he was accosted the moment he entered the kitchen.

"Boss!" Pablo cried, his little ratlike face screwed into a pained squint. "That lady's a beast!"

"A monster!" Angelo agreed, through a mouthful of food.

"Want some soup?" Tito asked from over by the stove, where he was stirring a steaming cauldron of rosemary potato chowder.

And really, this summed up Damien's dilemma. The Bandito Brothers were idiots and annoying and ate him out of house and home, and yet the aroma in the kitchen made him forget all that.

It was nose-wigglingly wonderful!

In no time, the despicably wicked Damien Black was on olfactory overload, drooling like a basset hound.

Damien, you see, did not cook.

He barely took time to eat.

He couldn't be bothered with things like nutrition and hydration and hunger pains.

He had work to do!

Banks to heist!

People to abduct!

And yet the aroma in his kitchen made his knees turn to jelly.

"She threw her breakfast at me!" Pablo complained.

"And her lunch at me!" Angelo added (although through the food in his mouth it sounded more like "Ah wunhhh ah eeee!").

Tito simply delivered a bowl of soup to Damien and asked, "Toast?" as Damien jelly-kneed into a chair.

Damien nodded, then held his long, pointy nose over the steaming bowl, his eyes drifting closed as he inhaled.

"You okay, boss?" Pablo asked (recognizing that there was something rather odd about his idol's behavior).

Damien snapped to. "No, you fool, I'm not!" He grabbed his spoon and jabbed it in Pablo's direction. "I had the wrong kid! How could I have followed the wrong kid? Four of those brats told me he owned a gecko, and I could tell he was hiding something when I asked him. But when I followed him, he *couldn't* have had the—"

It was at this point that Damien almost slipped. You see, the Bandito Brothers did not know exactly what it was that the boy and Sticky had that Damien wanted so badly. They only knew that Damien wanted whatever it was very, *very* badly.

So immediately Pablo's and Angelo's ears perked.

Their eyes sharpened.

Their breath caught.

They were finally going to find out what this was all about!

(Tito, meanwhile, buttered the toast.)

But Damien (much to Angelo and Pablo's dismay) caught himself in the nick of time. "—he didn't have my *stuff*," he said, then dug into his bowl of chowder.

Pablo and Angelo drooped, then watched Damien eat, wondering what his brilliant brain was plotting as he brooded in silence over his soup.

Damien was, indeed, plotting, but his situation with the boy had him at a great disadvantage. Children, you see, all looked alike to him. (That is, unless one had radically red hair or a brilliantly blond buzz cut. But even then, it was tough.) To Damien Black, distinguishing one child from another was like reading Chinese characters. The

67

vertical and horizontal lines of their faces all ran together in his mind. He had to really concentrate to distinguish one character from the other. And then, when several of them were thrown together, he got confused. They all just looked too similar.

Too annoyingly, confoundingly similar.

However, as he reached the bottom of his chowder, Damien (feeling now fortified and sur-prisingly refreshed) had the spark of a new idea.

And with it came the determination to try again.

He had to!

After all, he told himself, he now knew at least one thing more than he'd known the day before:

The boy was definitely *not* named Dave Sanchez.

Chapter 8
SILLY-CIRCUITING

Saving his sarcastic, fierce-faced teacher did not seem to Dave to be a good use of his superpowers.

(Or, in this case, superpow*er*.)

After all, superpowers should be used to fight evil, not save it, right? And according to Dave (and nearly every student at Geronimo Middle School), Ms. Veronica Krockle was most definitely evil.

So after considering Sticky's position on saving Ms. Krockle, Dave had only one thing to say to his sticky-toed friend:

"No way."

"Ah, *hombre*," Sticky said with a shake of his head. "Get your head out of mud pie."

"My head's not in mud pie," Dave snapped. "Ms. Krockle's a beast!"

"Don't I know," Sticky said with a snort.

"So why would I want to save her?"

Sticky studied the tips of his little gecko finger-nails. "To save yourself, *señor*."

"To save my—?" But then Dave understood. Damien Black wouldn't let a little thing like following the wrong boy stop him. Damien Black would return to school! And he'd keep coming back until . . . until Ms. Krockle was freed and could tell the police that he was a madman! The police would arrest him and this time they'd *keep* him behind bars!

Dave hated to admit it, but Sticky was right. Freeing Ms. Krockle was *his* ticket to freedom, too.

Now, while these gears were grinding in Dave's head, Sticky watched.

And waited.

And when he saw that Dave had reached the

inevitable conclusion, he gave Dave a sage little smile. "It may be ugly-buggly, *señor*, but it needs to be done."

Dave pushed off on his bike. "I can't believe it," he grumbled. "I've got to save *her?*"

"It's the right thing to do, *señor*."

"How can you *say* that?" Dave glanced over at the gecko on his shoulder.

"How can you of all people—well, of all *lizards*—say that?"

Sticky shrugged. "He'll kill her if you don't."

"Do I care? Do I really care? How many things has she killed? How many frogs has she cut up? She's evil, Sticky. She's mean."

"Don't I know," Sticky repeated. "But it's still the right thing to do."

"There has to be a better way," Dave grumbled. "There just has to!"

And so, to avoid facing the inevitable, Dave did *not* sneak out that night to rescue Ms. Veronica Krockle. Instead, he did his homework, did his chores, and went to bed before being told to.

I should, perhaps, point out that it wasn't fear holding him back.

It was the idea of rescuing Veronica Krockle.

Can you imagine a task so distasteful, so repulsive, so *counterintuitive* that you would do your homework *and* your chores *and* go straight to bed, all without being asked?

I thought not.

Now, it's a well-known fact that sleep has many healing properties. Most people are aware that sleep is the time for your body to make repairs, but it is also linked to fighting off cancers and bolstering memory and (believe it or not) losing weight.

As you can see, sleep is amazing, powerful stuff.

What sleep *cannot* do, however, is change reality.

It can only help you avoid it.

Until you wake up, that is.

And then you're right back where you were.

Dave did, in fact, wake up the next morning.

And Dave did, in fact, find himself in the midst of his same dilemma:

Should he save the Crocodile?

Or risk facing off with Damien Black?

But . . . wouldn't he also have to face off with Damien Black if he went to the mansion and set Ms. Krockle free?

Wasn't saving her like two hazards in one?

Well . . . not if he went to Damien's house while Damien was substituting at school. That might work.

Might.

More confused than ever, Dave did what any sensible boy of thirteen would do in such circumstances:

He buried his head under the covers.

"If you play hooky, *señor*," Sticky whispered through a slit in the blankets, "you will give yourself away."

"He can't keep coming back!" came Dave's muffled response.

"Sure he can, *señor*."

"The school's gotta figure out that he's a phony sooner or later!"

"Most likely later," Sticky grumbled. He crawled under the covers and began pulling on Dave's ear. "*Ándale, hombre!* Quit being such a *bobo* slowpoke."

Pulling on Dave's ear was something Sticky did out of desperation. Usually because, say, a boulder was about to smash them to mush. Or a snake was about to strike. Or Dave was looking left when a semitruck was bearing down on them from the right.

He also did it when Dave was being just plain stubborn.

As you might imagine, Dave hated it when Sticky pulled on his ear. Not only was it annoying, it reminded him of being a little kid.

Of being at the market with his grandma.

(His grandma who, it's sad to say, had long since died.)

"Stop that!" Dave said, flailing under the covers. "Leave me alone!"

Unfortunately for Dave, his mother (who had just opened his door) came rushing in and pulled back the covers. "*Mi'jo?*"

Sticky dived under the pillow while Dave bolted upright, caught his breath, and said, "Sorry. Bad dream."

Mrs. Sanchez looked at her son with concern. "Do you want to tell me about it?"

"Uh, no." He glanced at his clock. "Wow! Look at the time! I'm gonna be late!" And with that he got dressed and charged around the house, gathering his schoolwork, eating breakfast, brushing his teeth, and shouldering his bike.

"Later!" he called to his family on his way out the door.

"Have a good day!" his mom and dad called back.

"Say hi to your girlfriend," Evie singsonged.

So Dave zipped down the stairs (without running into or over anyone), zoomed to school (without getting a flat), arrived on time (or, more precisely, *early*), and discovered (by overhearing other students talking) that Dr. Schwarz was no longer substituting for Ms. Veronica Krockle.

"Yes!" Dave said, pumping his arm. And as he headed off to his first-period class, he felt good all over. "See, Mr. Doom-and-Gloom?" he whispered into his sweatshirt, where Sticky was hiding. "She's back, he's gone!"

"*Ay chihuahua,*" Sticky said with a little tisk. "Something's not right about this, *señor*. That was waaaaaaay too easy."

"Maybe *you're* what's not right, huh? Maybe it wasn't Damien Black to begin with!"

"Ay-ay-ay," Sticky said with a sigh, and really, what else was there to say? There was simply no talking to Dave when he was this happy. You see, the wiring in his thirteen-year-old brain had switched to silly-circuit, and the fact is, facts have no place in the snap-happy zapping of silly-circuits. Facts are simply powerless when a brain is in such a state, and nothing Sticky could say or do would pop Dave out of it.

What *would* pop his silly-circuit, however, was walking into science class.

Chapter 9
WALKING INTO SCIENCE CLASS

The teacher in the seventh-grade science class-room was not wearing a lab coat and black boots.

Nor was she wearing a brown tweed suit.

No, the teacher waiting patiently for her class to file in was just an ordinary, curly-haired, skirt-suited substitute, sporting a string of plastic pearls and a glittery I LOVE TEACHING pin.

"Wow, another sub?" Calvin Jones whispered as students huddled outside the science classroom. "The Croc must be on her deathbed or something."

Guilt jolted through Dave. Where *was* Ms. Krockle? He had seen traps and cages and dungeons inside Damien's monstrous mansion with

his own two eyes. He'd almost gotten caught in a couple of them! Was she in one?

And Sticky had told him about clammy walls in the labyrinth under the mansion where people could be shackled upside down until they cried for mercy. Sticky had told him about torture chambers filled with creaky, clanky killing (or contorting) contraptions! Sticky had told him . . . well, enough to make him shudder just thinking about going back to Raven Ridge.

But . . . what if Ms. Krockle *was* on a deathbed? A deathbed Damien Black had strapped her to!

What if, right now, that madman had her bound and gagged and was preparing to plunge a knife through her eeky-shrieky heart?

Okay, so he might have to plunge the knife in a bunch of times to find it, but what if she did actually have a heart, and piercing it with a knife did actually kill her?

This was the point at which the silly-circuiting in Dave's brain shorted out.

This was the point at which he started feeling like . . . a coward.

"Hey," Yasmine Branson said, nudging Fons Soto, "I am not sitting in someone else's seat again. That was totally awkward."

"Yeah," Eli Laslow said. "Me either."

And so the class filed in (dutifully taking their assigned seats) and sat quietly, gazing upon their new substitute (whose name, they learned from the flowery script on the whiteboard, was Ms. Dede Bartholomew).

"Good afternoon, class," the teacher said after the tardy bell rang, her double chin wiggling as she warbled. (She was, to dress it kindly, a plus-sized woman.) "I understand that yesterday's substitute was a bit . . . strange."

"You can say that again," students all around grumbled.

"There were apparently complaints that all he wanted to talk about was *geckos*?"

"Yeah," Fons muttered. "What was up with that?"

The substitute chuckled. "I could understand if he'd wanted to talk about *the* Gecko. After all, I've heard the Gecko goes to school here."

"Here?" Fons asked, sitting up.

This was followed by a flurry of questions and comments:

"Where'd you hear that?"

"Yeah. My dad said he's a field-worker!"

"No way! I heard he's in *high* school."

"Hey, if you could scale walls like he does, why would you even go to school? Or work in the fields?"

"I sure wouldn't."

Then Lily (who'd remained uncharacteristically quiet for two days now) said, "He does go to school. He goes to Yucca Middle School. I have a friend who knows him."

"You *do?*" everyone asked, turning to face her.

"She's lying," Yasmine Branson muttered with a scowl.

"Shut up," Lily said, half getting out of her seat.

"You're *always* lying," Yasmine said with a shrug.

Then Dave (whose brain had not quite adjusted to the sudden switch in circuitry) said, "Uh . . . I've heard the same thing."

Lily turned on him. "What—that I'm a liar?"

"No!" Dave sputtered, and turned a rosy red. "That he goes to Yucca."

"See?" Lily said, pointing an angry finger at Yasmine. "Who's a liar now, huh?"

Yasmine sneered, first at Dave, then at Lily. "Are you guys, like, going out or something?"

"Shut *up!*" Lily said, flying out of her seat.

Well! Just when it seemed the two girls would come to blows (or, at least, scratches), Ricky Zaragoza pointed at the ceiling and cried, "Look!"

And there was Tyler Mills's extra-credit gecko from the day before, hanging (rather miraculously) from the ceiling above their heads.

"That dweeb sub from yesterday would be going crazy right now!" Reuben laughed.

"Yeah. Ooooh, a gecko!" Fons said sarcastically.

Now, as all heads (including the sizeable sub's) cranked back to get a look at the gecko on the ceiling, all mouths dropped open. It is just a natural thing for a mouth to do when the head to which it's attached cranks backward.

And in the process of cranking heads and dropping jaws, Sticky (who'd been slyly watching the new substitute the whole time) got a lizard's-eye view inside the gaping mouth of Ms. Dede Bartholomew.

Suddenly his little gecko heart started clattering like castanets. *"Señor!"* he whispered up at Dave's ear. "The tooth! Look at the tooth!"

Sure enough, there it was, inside the gaping

mouth of the double-chinned, apple-cheeked (and, I might add, completely whiskerless) substitute: a sparkling gold molar.

It wasn't just any molar either.

It was the first molar behind the top left canine.

When Dave saw it, his skin did not just crawl. It crept and prickled and shivered and ran cold and then hot, and *then* crawled.

He now realized that he could no longer bury his head under the covers and hope Damien Black would go away.

Damien was like a recurring nightmare.

In one form or another, he would keep coming back.

And so it was that Dave decided:

It was time to return to Damien's monstrous mansion.

It was time to rescue Ms. Veronica Krockle.

Chapter 10
THE BOXING MATCH

The minute Dave realized that their female substitute with the curly hair and jostling jowls was, in fact, Damien Black wearing another (amazingly elaborate) disguise, a boxing match began inside his head.

In one corner: Stay in school until the end of the day.

In the other: Ditch.

If he left school early, he could ride up to Damien Black's mansion, sneak inside, rescue Ms. Krockle, and get out of there before Damien had had the chance to peel off his latex face. JAB, SMACK, BAM. With quick moves and fancy footwork, he could (perhaps) land a knockout in round one.

But rallying back from the other side were some simple, indisputable facts: Getting inside Damien's nightmarish mansion had never been easy. (JAB!) The place was *huge*. (PUNCH!) And he had no idea where Ms. Krockle was being held, or if she was even still alive. (BAM!)

Plus, Dave had never ditched school.

Not even one class period.

To the Sanchez family, ditching school was like stealing. "Just because you don't have to pay to go to school," his parents had told him, "doesn't mean it's not expensive. It's a gift that you must respect and appreciate."

So, despite all the reasons it would make his life easier, Dave did not feel right about cutting school, even if it was just for one class period.

It would be wrong.

Disrespectful.

A big, bad no-no.

So! This might well have been the knockout

store that had a window display that caused Dave to come skidding to a halt.

"What the *jalapeño* are you doing?" Sticky cried, for the sudden stop had practically thrown him off Dave's shoulder.

"I just had a brainstorm!" Dave cried, whipping the bike around.

"Uh-oh," Sticky said, which was completely out of character for the lizard. In normal circumstances (as well as stressful ones), Sticky would say, "Ay-ay." Or "Ay-ay-ay." Or "Ay-ay-ay-ay!" But "Uh-oh"?

Sticky was worried.

"Just stick to the plan, *señor*."

"What plan?" Dave said, heading inside the thrift store. "We don't have a plan!"

"Get up to that crazy *casa*, set her free, get out of there! That's the plan."

"That's no plan!" Dave said, opening the door and hurrying inside. "And even after we set her free, that's not going to stop Damien from coming back. And we might not recognize him next time!"

"So true," Sticky mused. He cocked his head, looking at Dave. "So what's *your* plan?" he whispered.

Dave hurried over to the window display, taking down a faded yellow sweatshirt that had large brown lettering across the chest spelling out YUCCA.

Yucca Middle School.

"*Señorrrrr!*" Sticky said. "This *is* a brainstorm."

Dave looked very pleased. "And," he said, picking up a worn, very traditional-looking black bandanna, "I'll use this to cover my nose and mouth. Like a field-worker keeping the dust out!"

Sticky gave him a sly grin. "Very confusing, *señor.*"

Dave grinned back. "Exactly."

So Dave paid for the sweatshirt and bandanna, then continued up to Raven Ridge, where he found a secluded spot in the forest on the outskirts of Damien Black's mansion to hide his bike and put on his disguise.

When he was ready, Sticky said, "*Híjole!* You look crazy good!"

And with that they sneaky-toed through the fearsome forest, determined to get in and out of Damien's mansion before the dastardly villain returned home.

Chapter 11
MEANWHILE, INSIDE THE MANSION

While Dave and Sticky were sneaky-toeing through the fearsome forest, the Bandito Brothers were inside the mansion drawing straws.

Now, by "drawing straws," I do not mean that they were broadening their artistic horizons by putting the finishing touches on, say, a still life of a bottle of soda with straws poking out of it.

No, by "drawing straws," I mean that they were choosing who would be saddled with the distasteful task of delivering a very late lunch to Ms. Veronica Krockle.

And although they were drawing straws, the Bandito Brothers were actually using weeds.

Weeds that were strewn (or clumped in great messy piles) around the mansion.

Weeds that were a seasonal mix of tall (and short) grasses, delectable dandelions, thorny thistles, wild arugula, and the occasional stick. Weeds that were used for the care and feeding of a buck-toothed burro named Rosie.

These weeds were (as you might imagine) an ongoing source of annoyance to Damien Black, but Rosie was part of the Bandito Brothers package. She was (aside from their well-callused feet) their sole source of transportation. And although she'd been banished by Damien Black to the outside of the house, as the old saying goes, when the cat's away, the mouse will play. (Or, in this case, when the villain's away, the mariachi band will play. And no, I am not referring to their instruments.)

Tito, in particular, had a soft spot for Rosie. So much so that he had (without Damien's knowledge or notice) sawed and chiseled and nailed and drilled away at a remote back entry until he had, at long last, installed . . .

A donkey door.

The donkey door was very much like a doggy door only considerably larger. In fact, it took up over half the door. And the flapping rubber shield that is typical on most doggy doors was, instead, a large black trash sack.

Which didn't always keep out biting bugs.

Or skittery squirrels.

Or . . . But no matter. After being guided through the donkey door a few times by Tito, Rosie got the hang of it and the donkey door served its purpose beautifully. The moment Damien was out of sight, Tito removed the cover (a sheet of plywood, painted to match the door), thereby giving Rosie full access to the house.

Or, at least, access to the part of the house that the Bandito Brothers had access to, which (in the scheme of the entire mansion) wasn't much.

Damien couldn't very well have them nosing through his gizmos and gadgets and priceless possessions! So he'd locked the Brothers out (with multi-linked, chunky-clunky, skeleton-keyed locks), or booby-trapped them out (with trapdoors and *boing*ing knives and slipknotted ropes), or scared them out (with pre-recorded groaning, whoooing, whooshing noises that no ghost-fearing mariachi band would dare investigate). These fellas were, undeniably, *thieves*, and if he couldn't get *rid* of them, he at least needed to *contain* them.

But let's get back to the drawing of straws, shall we?

The Brothers are, after all, about to determine whose job it will be to face the fierce and frightening Veronica Krockle.

"Over here, boys," Angelo called, holding three long (but pathetically limp) blades of grass. "We've got to get this done before Mr. Black gets home."

Pablo's mouth pulled down in a ratty-faced frown. "How stupid do you think I am?"

"Wadda ya mean?" Angelo asked.

"You're cheating."

"How am I cheating?" Angelo cried. "You're the one who always cheats!"

"How can I be cheating? I'm not even holding the grass."

"Well, why aren't you, huh? You never do anything around here!"

"Oh, and you do? You spend the whole day picking your nose."

"Shut up!"

"You shut up!"

Well! As you can see, these two Brothers found it hard to get much of anything done. Each task (no matter how small) had to be handled fairly and squarely, and Pablo and Angelo were always suspicious of one doing something crooked to the other.

By the end of each day, they were completely and utterly exhausted.

(After all, it takes considerable energy to argue over nothing.)

But although Angelo and Pablo were greatly concerned that they themselves not be shafted, they were more than happy to shaft Tito (which is how he wound up with all the jobs, dirty or otherwise). And since Angelo and Pablo had been arguing about who would deliver lunch to the ferocious Ms. Krockle since noon, Tito at last said, "I'll hold the straws."

"It's grass, stupid," Pablo snapped. "And you'll cheat!"

"I won't cheat."

"You always cheat!"

"No, I don't!"

"Yes, you do!"

And so it was that, in the end, the Brothers agreed that Rosie would be the one to hold the weeds.

Now, it's a well-known fact that burros

(bucktoothed or otherwise) don't hold weeds (or straws, for that matter).

They *chew* them.

Still. This was the only solution the Bandito Brothers could come up with, so as soon as Rosie had a good bunch of fresh weeds in her mouth (with strands sticking out this way and that), Pablo said, "Ready . . . steady . . . go!"

The Brothers shot forward, each snatching what they hoped was the longest strand.

Rosie didn't miss a munch.

"I win!" Pablo exclaimed, holding up a long stem with a mangled, dangly end.

"That part doesn't count!" Angelo said, pointing to the dangly part. "It's not sticking out!"

"So?"

"So it's hanging on by a thread!"

"But it *is* hanging on, isn't it?" Pablo said.

Angelo reached forward and snatched off the dangly end. "No!"

"Hey! Don't be stupid!"

"You don't be stupid, stupid!"

Meanwhile, Tito was looking at his little stumpy sprig, wondering how he always got the shortest weed. And while Pablo and Angelo battled it out (eventually ramping up their insults to "You're even stupider than a stupid torpedo filled with the stupidest stupidos ever!"), Tito fetched Veronica Krockle's tray of (by now cold and certainly stale) lunch and made his way up a wickedly winding staircase, down a dark and dank corridor, through a revolving door of palm fronds, past a chilling collection of Zulu masks, and up a final flight of very steep steps to the windowless tower where the feisty science teacher was waiting.

And oh my, was she ever waiting.

And not for lunch.

Oh no.

Ms. Veronica Krockle was waiting to pounce.

Chapter 12
STALKED

The doors of Damien's mansion ranged from standard issue (thirty-six-inch solid-core six-paneled jobbies) to completely customized (clonking, catapulting, whooshing, or air-locked units) to simply knobless or hingeless, or oddly shaped.

Additionally, there were doors that are best described as . . . alarming.

Now, by "alarming," I do not mean that the doors set off alarms. (Although almost every door that led inside the main part of the mansion did, in fact, do just that.)

No, this sort of alarming has nothing whatsoever to do with bells or buzzers or whistles (or snake rattles, for that matter). This sort of alarming has to do with the heebie-jeebie creepies you feel when coming face to face with, say, shrunken skulls dangling from a blood-red door.

Or tightly meshed blood-crusted tusks surrounding an ivory doorknob.

Or (as with the mansion's front door) a solid oak, heavily whitewashed monstrosity carved in the shape of a great, ghastly skull.

Ah, yes. Damien Black had a thing for devilish doors.

Doors that made you think twice about entering.

Doors that said, unmistakably, Keep out!

Go away!

Beat it, buster!

Dave Sanchez, however, had developed a knack for getting past Damien's devilish doors. Yes, they'd made him shudder or yelp or rub his poor, pummeled head, but (to Damien's complete exasperation) they had not stopped Dave from getting inside the mansion.

And so, while Veronica Krockle was plotting her way out (past the prisoner tower's six-inch-thick ironwood door), Sticky and Dave were sneaky-toeing through the forest toward the mansion discussing how to get *in*.

"You want to try the skull door?" Sticky asked.

Dave frowned. "I don't want to waste the time. It's bound to be locked."

"Through the bat cave, then?"

"You hate bats!" Dave said, then shook his head. "And he's probably put in new booby traps, don't you think? He knows we came in that way before."

Sticky snapped his little gecko fingers. "Say! The drawbridge may be down!"

"The drawbridge? What drawbridge?"

"Ay-ay," Sticky said with a twinkle in his little gecko eye. "The drawbridge that leads to another cave where he keeps his fishy-tailed car."

"Fishy-tailed car? What's a fishy-tailed car? And how many caves does he have?"

"Oh, lots of caves, *señor*. Lots." Sticky gave a little shrug. "And a fishy-tailed car is just a fishy-tailed car. It has long, pointy fins."

Now, as Dave and Sticky had been sneaky-toeing through the forest discussing doors (and fishy-tailed cars), they had been followed.

Silently.

Stealthily.

But now suddenly the stalker screamed, "Bwaa-ha-ha-caw! Bwaa-ha-ha-caw!"

"Ahhhh!" Dave squawked (in a very un-superhero-like manner), then cowered behind the wide, rough trunk of a gnarled pine tree. "Where is he?" he gasped, his heart pounding as he looked around madly for Damien Black.

"It wasn't him," Sticky called, but he had dived for cover inside Dave's sweatshirt and his little gecko heart was pounding.

"Then who was it? Or *what* was it?" Dave began searching the branches of the surrounding trees for speakers. They'd fallen for Damien's prerecorded voice before. Perhaps some of the large pinecones dangling from the branches above them were actually speakers. Speakers that were activated by movement in the forest. Speakers that—

"Bwaa-ha-ha-caw!"

"Ahhhh!" Dave cried again, only this time he noticed a large, black, oily-feathered raven staring at them from the gnarled branch of an adjacent pine.

He blinked at the bird.

The bird stared back.

"No . . . ," Dave whispered.

"What, *señor*?" Sticky asked, peeking out of the sweatshirt.

"Can birds—?"

"Bwaa-ha-ha-caw!" the bird shouted (in the

über-aggressive way that only ravens and crows can). "Bwaa-ha-ha-caw!"

"Ay-*ay*!" Sticky cried, diving for cover.

"Damien must have trained him," Dave whispered, staring at the bird with both fear and wonder.

"Keep him away!" Sticky cried. "Keep him away!"

Now, in most situations Sticky was fearless (or, it could be argued, cavalier and careless). But when it came to flapping beasts (like, say, bats or birds or oversized bugs), he became one sticky-toed scaredy-cat.

"Don't worry," Dave assured him, sidestepping away from the tree. "It's just a bird."

But as Dave hurried to put distance between him and the bird, the raven followed, calling, "Bwaa-ha-ha-ha-ha-ha-ha-caw! Bwaa-ha-ha-ha-ha-ha-ha-caw!" and soon another raven appeared.

And another.

And *another*.

"Bwaa-ha-ha-ha-ha-ha-ha-ha-caw!!" they all shouted, swooping around Dave as he hurried away from them. "Bwaa-ha-ha-ha-ha-ha-ha-ha-caw!!"

"Freaky *frijoles*!" Sticky cried. "Run!"

"What do you think I'm doing?" Dave cried.

"Well, run faster!" Sticky shouted, as there were now *eight* bwaa-ha-cawing birds swooping and swarming above them.

So Dave put the pedal to the metal (or, in this case, his sneakers to the dirt) and charged along the edge of the forest, keeping a shield of trees between him and the house in case Damien had installed surveillance cameras or motion-activated sleep darts or some other wicked doohickey to thwart people from approaching the mansion.

And so it was that Dave zigzagged through the outskirts of the forest, not really paying attention to where he was going as he attempted to escape the unkindness of ravens. (Which is, quite appro-priately, what it's called when ravens decide to gang up and chase after you, whether they bwaa-ha-ha or simply caw.)

"Get away from the trees!" Sticky cried from inside the sweatshirt. "I think they want you out of the forest."

And so Dave took the risk.

He stepped out of the forest.

Out of the shadows.

Into a bright, broad spotlight of sunshine.

He also, unfortunately, stepped smack-dab into a large, fresh pile of kneady-weedy donkey doo.

"Ewww!" Dave said, doing a little doo-doo dance away from the pile. "What's *that* doing here?"

Sticky, however, didn't give a sniff about a little donkey dung. The ravens were no longer chasing them (or bwaa-ha-cawing), but ahead of them was something odd.

Completely unexpected.

In a word, bizarre.

"Holy guacamole," Sticky gasped. "What is *that?*"

"It's not guacamole, that's for sure," Dave grumbled, still looking at his shoe.

"No," Sticky said, pointing straight ahead, "*that.*"

Sticky was pointing to one of the mansion's jutting walls.

It was expanding.

Pushing outward.

Growing, like a great black balloon.

And inside the balloon something was moving.

Something *alive*.

Chapter 13
ICKY-STICKY SYRUP

What came through the wall was not some agent of evil, or heat-seeking sleep darts, or boy-hunting hounds.

It was a burro.

A fuzzy-wuzzy bucktoothed burro.

One that immediately became preoccupied with the flittery-fluttering of a little yellow butterfly and did not notice Dave and Sticky standing a mere fifteen yards away.

"That's Rosie," Sticky whispered. "Which means those *bobos* banditos are still living here!"

"Wait," Dave said. "He let them put in a *donkey* door?"

Sticky shook his little gecko head. "It's *loco-berry* burritos, man."

They stared at the donkey door a moment longer, then looked at each other.

"You thinking what I'm thinking?" Dave asked.

"*Sí, señor,*" Sticky said with a grin. "No alarm, no creaky hinges, no catapults or bloody fangs. . . ." He nodded. "Even if those beany-brained boys are in there, it should be easy-sneezy to sneak inside."

Now, at this point, Tito was already on his way up to the prisoner tower. So when Dave and Sticky sneaky-toed up to the donkey door and peeked inside, the only Brothers left were Angelo and Pablo.

Dave and Sticky couldn't see them (as the donkey door had been installed in an old servants' entry off the side of the kitchen), but they could certainly hear them bickering. And after eaves-dropping for a few minutes, Dave whispered, "They're fighting about *weeds?*"

"You name it, *señor*, they will find some way to fight about it. Now *ándale*! That evil Mr. Black will be home soon!"

This was, in fact, an accurate (and appropriately ominous) statement, as at that very moment Damien Black was roaring up the winding road to Raven Ridge at hazardous speed, holding the wheel of his 1959 Cadillac Eldorado with one hand while ripping off the latex face of Ms. Dede Bartholomew with the other.

He was, to put it mildly, in a ferociously foul mood. He'd spent the day wearing a sweaty latex face, an itchy wig, a cheery pin, and nylons.

Nylons!

Itchy, pinchy, hair-pulling nylons!

And he'd gotten nowhere.

Nowhere!

Those sneaky-eyed, cagey kids were a nightmare!

A headache-inducing, stomach-churning, gut-gurgling nightmare!

Ah, poor Damien. He could handle thugs and thieves and devious businessmen.

Backstabbers and double-crossers (and even politicians!).

But children?

They were simply too much for him.

And so it was that Damien had made a mad, belly-jiggling dash for the exit when the dismissal bell rang at Geronimo Middle School. "Out of my way! Out of my way!" he'd shouted (in a curiously masculine voice), shoving through the teeming crowds of teens. And after continuing his mad dash over to his car (which was parked a cautious four blocks from school), he'd fired up his trio of ultra-bad Rochester carburetors and put the pedal to the Eldorado's metal (which, in this case, meant just that).

So, as you can see, Sticky's order to *"Ándale!"* was a wise one, indeed. Dave had, after all, stopped at the thrift store, pedaled up to Raven

Ridge (which, even for an experienced biker like Dave, was quite a trek), and been harassed and waylaid by bwaa-ha-cawing ravens.

Can you say tick-tock?

So without further delay, Dave eeeeeased through the donkey door, tiiiiippy-toed across the worn black-and-white flooring tiles, and sneeeeeaky-peeked a look around the pantry shelving into the kitchen.

There was no sign of Ms. Veronica Krockle.

Only Pablo and Angelo dousing each other with maple syrup.

"Stop that!" Pablo cried.

"You stop first!" Angelo shouted back.

"What are

they *doing?*" Dave whispered, for even in his most heated fights with Evie, he had never, not ever, poured syrup on her head.

Pablo doused Angelo with another glug of syrup as he yelled, "I'm not taking her food up, you hairy dog!"

"Yes, you are, you chintzy cheater!" Angelo shouted, glugging back.

"I think they're fighting about that scary *señorita!*" Sticky whispered.

Pablo suddenly lowered his syrup jug and looked around. "Hey . . . where's Tito?"

Angelo looked around, too. "I don't know, but the tray's gone."

Pablo snorted through his little ratty nose. "Well, good. He needs the exercise."

Angelo laughed. "Yeah. Ninety-nine steps. It'll take him all day."

Pablo plopped down in a tattered vinyl kitchen-table chair. "I hate those creepy masks in that tunnel. The eyes." He shuddered. "Do you think they're really alive?"

Angelo plopped down across from him and started wiping the syrup off his face and arms. "Don't be stupid. How could they be alive, huh?"

"Hey!" Pablo said, sitting up straighter. "I'm not stupid, you're stupid!"

"Shut up! You're stupider than the stupidest stupid ever!"

And so they were off again, outdoing each other's insult, oblivious to the fact that they'd just given away Ms. Veronica Krockle's location.

"She's in the tower!" Sticky whispered into Dave's ear.

"How do we get there?" Dave whispered back.

"Up ninety-nine rickety steps and through a creepy tunnel of masks. *Oooor*"—he tapped his little gecko chin thoughtfully—"we could use the stinky socks chute."

"The stinky socks chute?" Dave pulled a face. "I'll take the ninety-nine steps."

Sticky arched a hairless eyebrow. "I don't think so, *señor*."

"Why?"

Sticky peeked around the corner at Pablo and Angelo (whose argument had ramped up to "Well, you're stupider than the stupidest stupid sauce *inside* the dumbest dumb bomb ever, and every time you explode, stupid sauce splats all over the wall!"). He eyed Dave. "Because to get to the ninety-nine steps, you first have to get past those two. And what if Tito is on his way down?"

"Can't we just go up the outside of the house?"

Sticky shook his head. "No windows in the tower."

"So where's the laundry chute?" Dave whispered

(for he'd figured out that's what the stinky socks chute must be).

Sticky pointed to an open room located across a wide common area. "In there."

It was clear that crossing over this wide common area would put them in full view of Pablo and Angelo. Even in the heat of their argument, the two Brothers would surely spot a boy in a yellow sweatshirt sneaking by.

But then Dave noticed that spanning the ceiling above the wide common area was a large wooden beam. One that would (at least partially) conceal them if they walked across the ceiling.

Sticky and Dave exchanged glances, and without a word, Dave (who still had the Wall-Walker ingot in the powerband) scampered up the wall and started across the ceiling.

Now, it's frightening enough to be trespassing in a madman's mansion, walking across the ceiling like a giant yellow gecko while two angry men sporting bandoliers and bad attitudes (not to mention jugs of syrup) are within striking distance. But nothing, I promise you, *nothing* will make you lose your grip quicker than Damien Black's voice booming through the room.

"Where are you buffoons?" the angry treasure hunter shouted from a distant chamber.

Pablo and Angelo frantically began wiping up syrup.

"Answer me!" bellowed Damien's approaching voice.

"*Ándale!*" Sticky whispered, because Dave had, quite simply, frozen in place.

"H-h-here, boss!" Angelo called, and with that Dave kicked into gear, geckoing across the rest of the ceiling to the safety of the adjacent service room.

Almost immediately, Damien entered the kitchen area. "Where's your brother!" he bellowed, not even noticing that there was icky-sticky syrup everywhere.

"H-h-he's not our brother," Angelo said.

"Do I CARE? Where is he?"

"Checking on the prisoner," Pablo replied. "What happened, boss?"

"I'm done," Damien snapped. "Come on. Let's get rid of her."

So as the two Brothers hurried to follow Damien up ninety-nine rickety steps, Dave worked his way through a pile of putrefying socks and zippy-toed straight up the laundry chute, racing to reach Ms. Veronica Krockle before Damien could kill her.

Chapter 14
FREEDOM!

Up in the tower, Ms. Veronica Krockle had no idea that anyone (and certainly not one of her students) was on his way to rescue her from her windowless prison. How could she? She didn't even know where she was, or why she'd been abducted and tortured. All she knew was that she wanted *out*.

I should point out that she had not been tortured in the traditional sense. Damien had not clamped her to any of his cranking, crunching, jabbing, jostling (or, for that matter, tickling) devices. He hadn't hung her upside down by her ankles or trapped her inside his terrifying terrarium of tarantulas.

No, she had been tortured by something much worse. You see, to Ms. Veronica Krockle, there was no agony more excruciating, no torture more intolerable, no assault more savage than the raw, throbbing pain of stupidity.

"How could I have let those blockheads capture me?" she muttered (for the only people she had actually seen were the Bandito Brothers). "Who *are* they? What do they want?" (Secretly, she feared they were former students of hers, extracting a long-awaited revenge.)

Now, you may be wondering how Ms. Veronica Krockle could be muttering when the Bandito Brothers had, in fact, bound and gagged her with duct tape.

Lots and lots of duct tape.

Well, I'll tell you how:

Ms. Veronica Krockle had slobbered her way out.

It wasn't that her spit was acidic, or toxic, or

special in any way. It was (like all spit) simply wet (and, okay, maybe a little foamy). But the wetness of her spit eventually broke down the extreme stickiness of the tape across her mouth, and once her mouth was free, her *teeth* were free, and after that? Oh my—there was no stopping her. She ripped and tore (and, yes, slobbered) her way out of the tape's sticky bondage until she was at last free from the wooden chair to which she'd been bound.

And now she was able to move about the room.

Able to lie in wait behind the door.

Able to clonk the next idiot to enter!

That idiot was, of course, Tito. And when she heard him begin to unlock the thick iron-wood door, Ms. Veronica Krockle's hardened heart skipped a ferocious beat.

When the heavy metal security latches outside the room went CLONK, CLONK, CLONK,

Ms. Veronica Krockle hefted the chair overhead.

When the door *squeeeee-eee-eeeaked* open, Ms. Veronica Krockle held her breath.

Her eyes grew steely.

And when Tito entered the room, CRAAAAAAAACK, CRUNCH, CLATTER-CLATTER-clatter-clatter, Ms. Veronica Krockle whacked him over his head with the chair.

Dazed and (additionally) confused, Tito staggered for a few steps, dropped the tray of food, but did not go down. (It is, after all, impossible to knock out a rock.)

But dazed and confused was all Ms. Veronica Krockle needed. Before Tito could react, she'd scooped up a runaway apple (as she was, at this point, starving), dashed out, slammed the door closed, and shoved in the security latches, locking Tito inside the room.

"Freedom!" she cried (with a laugh that

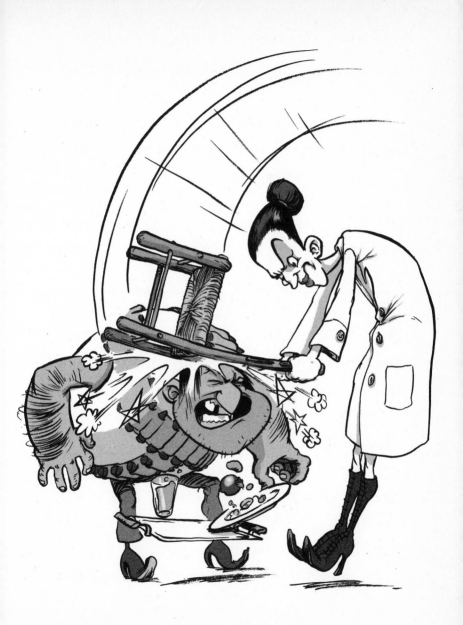

sounded eerily like "Bwaa-ha-ha"). But after she had descended the tower's steps and looked around, she had no idea which way to go.

She hurried to the left but had to stop when she came upon a wide hole in the floor. Above the hole, a thick, knotted rope came out of the wall and looped over a paddle-wheeled pulley, then dangled into the hole and down, down down into a deep, dark abyss.

"How far down does this go?" she gasped, then did a rapid-fire munch-munch-munch-slurp-crunch of the apple and tossed the core into the abyss.

She quit chewing, cupped an ear, and waited.

And waited.

And *waited*.

No sound came up the shaft.

At last, she swallowed the apple in her mouth, shuddered, and backed away.

But after running in the opposite direction,

she soon found herself in a cramped corridor of Zulu masks.

Now, perhaps when you think of a Zulu mask, you imagine a large, crudely carved, semi-rectangular wooden mask with holes for eyes, warrior markings, and a menacing expression.

This would, after all, be a reasonable thing to imagine.

And these masks did, indeed, have those features, but they also had coarse bursts of long, angry hair.

And eyes.

Eye*balls*, actually.

Eyeballs that seemed to be tracking each and every one of Ms. Veronica Krockle's moves.

The Zulu masks were on both sides of the corridor, and as Veronica Krockle tiptoed through this tunnel of mad-eyed masks, her head whipped from side to side, trying to follow all the eyes following her. "What madman is behind this?" she gasped, for in her growly gut she knew that the Bandito Brothers could not possibly be the masterminds of this ghastly sight.

This was all much too bizarre for those simpletons.

Much too . . . *twisted*.

Then she heard footsteps approaching.

Hard-heeled, *angry* footsteps.

Immediately she knew it wasn't one of the clowns who'd bound and gagged her. From the sound of his footsteps, she quickly sensed that whoever it was was dangerous.

Now, it's a well-known fact that when panic strikes, the mind pulls in its welcome mat, drops the blinds, and hides. And pounding on the door and crying, "Help! Emergency!" has little effect. You're out in the cold.

Left in the dark.

In a word, doomed.

So (feeling both panicked and doomed) Ms.

Veronica Krockle did the only thing she could think to do.

She slapped herself against the wall, held her breath, and widened her eyes, hoping (almost praying) that she'd be mistaken for a Zulu mask.

Chapter 15
UNMASKED

The simple (although admittedly unkind) truth is that Ms. Veronica Krockle's fearsome face blended in quite nicely with the Zulu masks. And perhaps she would have gotten away with hiding among them had it not been for one inconvenient fact:

She had a body.

Which was, unfortunately for her, something none of the other Zulu masks had.

And so when Damien Black's hard-heeled feet rounded the corner (followed by the breathless Angelo and Pablo), he immediately recognized that there was something not quite right in the Zulu corridor.

One of his masks had grown a body.

A very un-Zulu-like body.

One wearing a white lab coat.

And black high-heeled boots.

He slowed as he approached, until he was standing directly in front of Ms. Veronica Krockle.

He looked into her wide, dark eyes.

He looked some more.

Despite Damien's quick, diabolical mind, it took some time for it to really register with him that this fierce and menacing face was *not* a Zulu, but his prisoner.

"Fools!" he hissed, throwing a withering look at Pablo and Angelo. "You let her escape!"

The two Brothers immediately pounced, grabbing Ms. Veronica Krockle by her wiry arms.

"We got her, boss! We got her!" Angelo cried. "She won't get away!"

"It's Tito's fault!" Pablo said with a ratty nod of the nose. "He's always messing up!"

"Shut up, you fools!" Damien hissed. "Don't you see what you've done?"

"We didn't do anything, boss! We *captured* her!" Angelo cried, tightening his grip on Veronica Krockle.

"That's right, sir. See? We've secured the prisoner," Pablo said (trying hard to sound both intelligent and in charge).

"Shut *up*," Damien cried, pulling at his long, oily hair.

Now, he wasn't pulling his hair because Pablo and Angelo were being bumbling, blundering idiots.

He was used to that.

And it wasn't because it's extremely annoying to have a moron try to sound smart.

He was used to that, too.

It was because of a problem much, much bigger than those small annoyances.

A problem much *graver*.

You see (unbeknownst to Dave), Damien had been planning to simply conk Ms. Veronica Krockle over the head and return her to the schoolyard.

Easy come, easy go.

But now his prisoner, his captive, his detainee had *seen* him.

Which meant she could ID him.

And if she could ID him, he couldn't just conk her out again and return her to school.

Now he had to kill her.

You may well be wondering how Ms. Veronica Krockle could take the terror of being face to fearsome face with the deadly, diabolical Damien Black.

Perhaps you're imagining her shaking in her high-heeled boots.

Or flashing through each moment of her science-teacher life.

But Ms. Veronica Krockle was neither shaking nor flashing.

She was, in fact, melting.

Now, by "melting," I do not mean turning into a pool of icky-sticky goo. By "melting," I mean that Ms. Veronica Krockle was softening on the inside. Her hard-hearted view, her rigid dislikes, her fortified contempt of, well, people in general were suddenly . . . missing. And in their place was a strange and frightening soft-ness.

A billowy, feathery *peace*.

Why?

Because Ms. Veronica Krockle had never seen eyes as deep or as dark as Damien's.

They were like pools of ink.

Or orbs of onyx.

Or . . .

She couldn't decide. Actually, she couldn't (for perhaps the first time in her life) *think*.

It wasn't fear that was keeping her from func-tioning.

Oh no.

It was a strange new emotion in her heart.

She had never in her life seen a man so breathtakingly handsome.

So dashing or commanding.

So, in a word, *hot*.

No, Ms. Veronica Krockle was most definitely *not* shaking in her high-heeled boots.

She was, instead, falling in love.

Chapter 16
CONVERGENCE OF EVIL

While Veronica Krockle was falling in love with Damien, and Damien was deciding how best to kill her, Dave and Sticky were watching this convergence of evil through a metal grating located

(as chance would have it) directly behind a pair of shiny black high-heeled boots.

Why was Dave behind a metal grating and not peeking out of, say, a laundry chute door?

Quite simply, Damien never changed his stinky socks on his way to the prisoner tower, so why put in a door? (He changed his socks infrequently enough to begin with, so expecting him to consider toe jam while on his way to securing a prisoner would be, at best, unrealistic.)

So after exiting the laundry chute on the third floor, Sticky had directed Dave through a maze of doors (both solid-core and trap), then inside patchy ventilation ductwork that ran this way and that until they were finally behind the Zulu mask tunnel. (Sticky had, to Dave's amazement, not taken one wrong turn.)

As speedy as they'd been, they hadn't been fast enough. And although Ms. Krockle was technically within reach, Dave couldn't very well open the grating and yank her inside the ventilation space by her high-heeled boots. Besides the very real possibility that she would kick and scream and poke out his eye with those yiky-spiky heels, there really wasn't room for her inside the ductwork. It was quite cramped to begin with, and even if he could manage to yank her inside without losing an eye, Damien Black would surely follow.

The duct would be plugged like it'd gotten a slug of demented cement.

Just thinking about it gave Dave a heart-hammering case of claustrophobia. So instead of making a move, he stayed crouched behind those high-heeled boots, taking deep, calming breaths as he tried to figure out what to do next.

Meanwhile, out in the Zulu corridor, Ms. Veronica Krockle couldn't tear her eyes away from Damien. Likewise, Damien still didn't know what to do with Veronica Krockle.

"The dragon pit!" Angelo whispered. "Take her there!"

"Shut up, you fool!" Damien hissed, his eyes locked on Veronica Krockle.

"I know, boss!" Pablo said with a sneer. "Take her to the dungeon of death!"

"Shut *up*," Damien hissed again, his eyes still locked on his prisoner.

"I know! The barracuda tank!" Angelo cried.

Damien turned to face Angelo. "WHAT PART OF '*SHUT UP*' DON'T YOU UNDERSTAND?"

The sound was so fierce and raw with anger (and, I'm afraid, lunchtime sardine breath) that the walls rattled (causing Zulu eyes to dart back and forth, up and down, all around).

Angelo jumped back.

Pablo cowered.

But at the same time (as if at long last released from its cage), Ms. Veronica Krockle's heart fluttered and stuttered, then soared.

Her eyelids drooped as she inhaled the treasure hunter's musky intensity (and alluring sardine breath).

And then, for the first time in her hard-hearted life, Ms. Veronica Krockle went wobbly in the knees.

"Help! Help!" came Tito's muffled cry from the tower room (as even he had heard Damien's wall-shaking shouting).

Damien threw his hands into the air. "I'm surrounded by idiots!" he seethed. "Imbeciles and idiots!"

And with those words, the magic was complete. Ms. Veronica Krockle had, at long last, found someone who could truly understand how she felt each and every day of her tortured teacher life. She was now wholly and totally under his spell.

"Get your brother," Damien snarled at Pablo and Angelo, "then go back to your quarters and *stay* there!"

"But, boss—"

"Go!"

"But—"

"GO!"

Pablo and Angelo shuffled away, grumbling, "He's *not* our brother."

The instant the two Brothers (not to be confused with brothers) started up the steps to the windowless tower, Damien did what any cold-hearted captor would do:

He clonked his prisoner over her starry-eyed head (once again using his pygmy hippo club).

Then he flung her over his shoulder and hurried toward the Bottomless Shaft.

Chapter 17
BOMBS AWAY!

There was no need for Damien to have conked Veronica Krockle over her starry-eyed head.

She would have followed him anywhere.

But there she was, flung like a sack of potatoes over Damien's shoulder, on her way to the Bottomless Shaft as Dave removed the metal grate and poked his nose into the Zulu corridor.

"There they go, *señor!*" Sticky whispered, pointing at the vanishing figures.

Now, it would have been logical for Damien Black to have simply flung the unconscious science teacher down the shaft. After all, the object was to kill her, right?

However, when it comes to the dastardly,

demented mind of Damien Black, logic is not always the linchpin of reasoning.

In other words, he sometimes does things that are puzzling.

Bamboozling.

Odd, illogical, and unnecessary.

One might almost suspect that the dastardly, demented Damien Black was a little trigger-shy when it came to actually *killing* someone.

But that would be a silly thing to suspect, given his track record of diabolical deeds, now wouldn't it?

It would be wiser (and decidedly more logical) to suspect that the devilish Damien Black simply relished the experience and wanted to prolong the process.

Enjoy the agony.

Savor each and every torturous moment.

Ah, yes. Anyone would agree. This behavior was simply reflective of the villain's mental state, as opposed to, say, a soft spot in his devilishly diabolical heart.

But let's get back to the pointy point, shall we? Which is that Damien did not simply chuck Veronica Krockle into the shaft and let her splat to her death. Instead, like a fiendish Tarzan in a flapping black coat, he leapt onto the knotted rope, swinging himself and his spiky-heeled Jane aboard. Then, *thump-wump-BUMP*, *thump-wump-BUMP*, he rode the rope down, down, down into the darkness below.

The instant Damien was gone, Dave crawled out of the ductwork and hurried toward the shaft. Unfortunately, the Bandito Brothers were descending the tower steps as Dave and Sticky went by.

"Hey!" Pablo cried. "It's the boy!"

"Get him!" Angelo shouted, waddling down the steps.

"*Ándale, hombre!*" Sticky cried, whipping the

fabric of Dave's sweatshirt like the reins of a horse.

Now, Sticky's command (and the whipping) was quite unnecessary, as Dave had already *ándale*d. It was also quite unfortunate, as there's only one voice like Sticky's, and that is (you guessed it) Sticky's.

"Sticky!" Tito squealed. "Wait up, little buddy!"

Dave wasn't about to wait up. Oh no. He raced full speed ahead. But when he reached the hole in the floor, he instantly reeled back. "How far down does that go?" he gasped.

"You have no choice, *señor*! Get on the rope!"

"*Where* does it go?"

"I have no idea, *señor*! Just go!"

Dave glanced over his shoulder. The Bandito Brothers were closing in fast. He could see the hairs sticking out of Angelo's arms. He could see a drip glistening on the edge of Pablo's pointy nose.

And there was the frightening twinkle in Tito's eyes (not to mention the alarmingly goofy grin spread from cheek to stubbly cheek).

"Now!" Sticky cried.

And so Dave jumped onto the knotted rope and went . . .

Nowhere.

"Ah!" he warbled. "How do I make this thing go?"

The Bandito Brothers were upon them now, and rather than waste any more time on the rope, Dave took a leap of faith (as he was never entirely sure the wristband's powers would actually work) and dived for the far wall of the shaft.

"Gecko Power is *asombrrrrroso!*" Sticky cried as they scurried down the wall of the shaft.

Above them, the Bandito Brothers were beside themselves with wonder.

They were blinking and bug-eyeing and sputtering at the mouth.

Their eyebrows were knitting and crossing and flying around all over their foreheads.

They were, in short, freaking out.

"Did you see that?" they all asked each other. "How did he *do* that?"

Now, they had, in fact, seen Dave scale walls before, but it had always been in an upward direction. In an it-could-have-been-a-rock-climber fashion. Mere mortals have, after all, scaled tall buildings armed with nothing more than their fingers and toes (and, okay, a hearty dose of insanity).

But going headfirst *down* a wall?

Even Tito recognized that this was an impossible feat.

"Maybe the lizard and the boy are switched!" Angelo said, his eyes growing wide. "Maybe the boy's in the lizard's body and the lizard's in the boy's body."

This seemed to snap Pablo out of his trance.

His squinty eyes pinched down as he looked at Angelo. "That's the stupidest thing I've ever heard. It's probably just suction cups."

"Suction cups?" Angelo shot back. "Did *you* see suction cups? No? Well, see? That makes *you* the stupidest thing ever!"

"Oh yeah? Well, you're even stupider than—"

"Uh . . . they're getting away?" Tito said, scratching the side of his big, round head as he looked down the shaft.

Angelo and Pablo locked eyes and the exact same thought double-crossed both their minds:

Whoever caught the boy would surely become Damien's right-hand man!

Not thinking beyond that, they both lunged for (and wrapped themselves around) the rope (and each other).

Of course, the rope didn't thump-wump-BUMP for them either. And after going nowhere for a full minute, they began screeching at Tito (who was preoccupied with two little chunks of grassy dirt that he'd found near the edge). "What are you doing, you idiot!" they cried. "Quit playing with dirt and help us!"

So Tito dropped the dirt and squatted at the edge of the Bottomless Shaft. "Why'd you get on the rope?" he asked, stretching out to reel them in. "Sticky's friend couldn't make it work."

Pablo stared at him for a moment, then snapped, "We thought he wasn't heavy enough, okay, stupid? Now stretch! Help us off of here!"

So Tito (simple soul that he was) leaned out farther.

And farther.

And *farther*.

Until he simply tumbled over the edge and fell headlong into the vast darkness below.

Chapter 18
BOTTOM OF THE BOTTOMLESS SHAFT

There was, of course, a bottom to the Bottomless Shaft. And it wasn't a hard cement pad or a plot of bone-crushing dirt.

It was feathers.

Floufy, poufy, soft and woufy feathers.

The kind that float forever in the air if you blow on them.

The kind that you can smash way down, then watch flouf way up.

The kind that feel like a cloud when you fall into them.

Now, these floufy, poufy, soft and woufy feathers were in an enormous chicken-wire container (which was either filled to the poufy-woufy top or only about half full, depending on whether something like, say, a large boulder-brained Bandito Brother had just landed).

But why the feathers?

Or, more curiously (considering the skyrocketing price of down on the international market), how had Damien managed to obtain such an enormous supply?

The answer is quite simple:

Damien owned geese.

Lots and lots of honking, squonking, angry-beaked geese.

And why did Damien own these honking, squonking, angry-beaked geese?

Because they were what Damien fed his dragon.

His sharp-clawed, hinged-jawed, ravenous Komodo dragon.

(Picture, if you will, a ten-foot, two-hundred-pound carnivorous lizard with deadly claws, serrated teeth, a monstrous appetite, and hot, beastly breath. That picture is as close as you should ever get to Damien's prized and pampered pet. The real thing could tear you to shreds in three-point-four seconds flat.)

But let's get back to the geese, shall we?

Geese eat things like weeds and snails, and they molt every six weeks when they're growing.

Every six weeks!

Can you imagine all the shedding feathers? Can you just see feathers floufing around all over the place?

And since Damien had lots and lots of geese, and the geese were always growing (as they rarely made it to full size before being fed to the dragon), the goose cave had been a constant blizzard of feathers.

Until, that is, Damien built the feather cage and got busy with a leaf blower.

Not only did it tidy things up dramatically, but

Damien also found that wielding the blower was amazingly therapeutic. The rev of the motor, the blast of air, the power to drive things in a direction *he* determined . . . it made him feel happy.

In control.

Satisfied.

(It was, perhaps, as close to gardening as he would ever come.)

Now, although the ten-foot cage of feathers was not a safety necessity when riding the knotted rope down the shaft, it was a billowy bonus, and Damien would often let go of the rope and land with an arm-flung "Aaaaaaah!" simply for the soul-soothing softness of it all.

This time, however, Damien's trip down the shaft was entirely business. Toward the end of the knotty rope ride, Damien shoved down a long lever on the wall, which lowered a landing platform that had an attached slide. Once he'd landed, he secured the rope (as he was aware that

the Brothers might, once again, try to defy his orders), then slid with his conked-out prisoner to the ground below, bypassing the feather pit altogether.

At the bottom of the slide, Damien pressed another lever to retract the landing platform. Then he whooshed through his gaggle of geese (which is what a group of honking, squonking geese is called, whether they're molting or not) and began muttering to himself as he ascended the five steep stone steps that led up to a cobblestone walkway. "It'll be over in no time," he hissed, but his normally quick and determined steps seemed to be dragging. "She's out cold," he muttered. "She'll never know what bit her."

Meanwhile, Dave and Sticky were nearing the bottom of the shaft when Tito came hurtling past them like a bandoliered boulder, crying, "Wheeeeeeeeee-hee-hee-hee-hee! Wheeeeeeeeeee-hee-hee-hee-hee!"

(Obviously he didn't understand the severity of the situation, and that he might very well have ended his days with a wicked, boulder-cracking splat.)

But (as you already know) Tito did not land with a wicked splat. He landed with a WOOOOUF, POOOOOOOOOOOOOUF! as the feathers beneath him compressed and those to the sides went billowing into the air.

Dave and Sticky had just reached the bottom of the shaft when Tito landed. "Puffy-huffy *plumas!*" Sticky cried, swatting feathers from the air in front of his face. "What will that *loco lobo* think of next?"

"What's with all the geese?" Dave said, as he could now clearly see (and hear) the molting birds.

"Dragon dinner," Sticky said with a shudder.

Dave shuddered, too, as he had once witnessed the feeding of the Komodo dragon, but his shudder was cut short by an echoing "AAAAAAA-AAHHHHHHHHH!" hurtling down the shaft along with the hair-raised body of Angelo.

Angelo landed with a (somewhat smaller) WOOOOUF, POOOOOOOOOOOOOUF next to Tito and immediately began flailing in the feathers. "Am I dead? What is this?"

"It's a pillow!" came Tito's muffled voice. "Let's have a pillow fight!"

"You idiot!" Angelo screamed, feathers tickling his nose. "How do we get—AAAAAAAAH-CHOOOOOOOO! AAAAAH-CHOOOOOO! AAAAAAH-CHOOOOOOOO!—out of here?"

"*Ándale, hombre,*" Sticky whispered in Dave's ear. "Before they see us."

So Dave skirted around the feather cage and soon found himself in an enormous cave, being honked at by the gaggle of geese. Through the geese was a rickety wooden bridge leading across a marshy area to an island. And on the other side of the island, shining through the bars of a large wrought-iron gate, was a warm, welcoming pool of sunshine.

Dave realized this was an exit.

An escape hatch.

A way out of the mansion's madness.

Yet he also knew he had a job to finish. So he moved on, trying to determine which way Damien might have taken Ms. Krockle.

Ahead of them was the open mouth of a three-foot tube that stuck out of the cave wall by a few feet like a gigantic, compressed, foil-covered Slinky.

"What is *that?*" Dave asked.

"Beats me, *señor,*" Sticky replied. "I've never been here before." He cocked an eye at Dave. "But I don't like the looks of it."

Dave nodded. The tube gave him the heebie-jeebies, too, although he couldn't say why. "So that way, you think?" Dave said, pointing to some steep steps and a cobblestone pathway.

Sticky gave a somber nod. *"Sí, señor."*

And so Dave took a deep breath and followed the cobblestones, knowing full well that he was moving deeper and deeper into the twisted darkness of Damien's lair.

Chapter 19
VARANUS KOMODOENSIS

Whenever he fed his prized Komodo a special treat (be it hog or, say, human), Damien Black introduced the meal into the dragon pit via trapdoor, or wicker cage, or slippery slide, or catapult (to mention a few). This gave him the opportunity to activate the release of the meal himself and enjoy a live-action showdown from the comfort of a skybox.

Yes, I said "skybox."

However, by "skybox," I do not mean a large, glass-faced room for bird's-eye viewing by dozens of spectators. By "skybox," I mean a large, glass-faced room for bird's-eye viewing by *one*.

You see, Damien's skybox had but a single

chair. It was a high-back executive swivel chair (black, of course), with padded armrests, adjustable lumbar support, pneumatic seat adjustments, and a locking tilt control.

Damien had found it to be perfect except that the casters were crunchy and slow across the cement floor of his skybox. So (rather than install carpeting) he removed the stock casters and installed four-inch rubberized (and deeply treaded) replacements (which he, of course, made himself). These new wheels gave him speed, traction, and the bonus of extra height for superior viewing across the control console.

Ah, yes. The control console. This was a shiny black surface that was neatly contoured to the curve of the viewing window and had all the buttons and levers and gizmos that controlled (among other things) the trapdoors, wicker cages, slippery slides, and catapults. (It also contained a small mix board for the room's surround sound, as

Damien liked to boost the bass and add a little re-verb once the action got under way—squeals and screams being so much more intense with a little audio processing thrown in.)

Like a traditional skybox, Damien's did have a wet bar, although (quite untraditionally) it held no booze. Instead, there were bottles of deeply chilled sparkling Armenian pomegranate juice (Damien's favorite thirst-quenching beverage).

The skybox was one of Damien's favorite rooms. In it, he felt a grand sense of power and control.

It was like his own private balcony at Carnage-y Hall.

Now, it was Damien's intention to load the cat-scratch teacher into the catapult (or maybe the slide?) and then dash up to his skybox to start the show. But (despite all the muttering he'd done to himself) there was one pesky thing giving him pause.

His prisoner was a woman.

A very . . . *attractive* woman.

One whose eyes had shown no fear.

Not even a trace.

Damien couldn't make sense of this.

Couldn't reconcile it.

Weren't women blithering, blubbering bundles of nerves?

Didn't they faint at the mere sight of a mouse?

Screech at the fluttery flap of a bat?

And yet back in the Zulu corridor he had given her his best nerve-shattering stare for a full minute and she hadn't flinched.

Hadn't even blinked.

"Quit it, you fool!" he muttered to himself. "It has to be done!" And right then and there, he decided to use the catapult.

It would be quick.

Absolute.

And irreversible.

Unfortunately for Damien, at the exact moment of his newfound resolve, Ms. Veronica Krockle stirred.

"Drat!" he muttered, as this could only mean one thing:

She was coming to.

Now, in his skybox, Damien kept another nontraditional skybox provision:

A coffin.

It was a simple wooden model (made, of course, by Damien himself). But this particular coffin was not intended (as you might expect) for the storage of bodies. Instead, it stored emergency supplies: rope and handcuffs and blindfolds and blowtorches—that sort of thing.

So when Ms. Veronica Krockle began to come to, Damien made the questionable decision to haul her up to the skybox so he could first bind her and blindfold her and *then* catapult her.

(It was, he reasoned, not much of a delay, but

you and I might suspect that his trigger finger had developed a really strange cramp. Perhaps even paralysis.)

Regardless, once in the skybox, Damien plopped his prisoner in his custom-castered chair and began ransacking the coffin for rope and a blindfold.

Veronica Krockle was, however, more conscious than he knew. And after slyly viewing his backside for a few moments, she happened to notice the dragon in the pit below. "Oh!" she gasped, leaning closer to the window. *"Varanus komodoensis."* She swiveled to face Damien. "He's magnificent!"

Damien stared at her, stunned.

She knew the genus and species of his Komodo dragon?

And she thought he was magnificent?

And that look on her face . . . what did that *mean*?

Poor Damien. This was all simply too much for him to process.

And so he did the only thing he could think to do:

He conked her on the head again (with his pygmy hippo club, of course).

Meanwhile, Sticky and Dave had been following the cobblestone pathway, coming to fork after fork in the road, going deeper and deeper into Damien's subterranean lair.

But as they approached the next fork and Dave was about to say, "We are totally lost!" Sticky whispered, "*Señor!* I know where we are!"

"You do?" Dave asked.

Sticky pointed to one blood-red cobblestone on the path to the right. "Thataway to the skybox!"

"He's got a *skybox?*"

"*Sí, señor.* It's his control center. It's how he gets . . . ay-ay, how do you say . . . *food* into the pit." He shuddered. "The sounds are *horroroso*."

The whisper of Sticky's voice caused a shiver

to shinny up Dave's spine. And in his heart of hearts he knew it was time to turn around.

Time to go home.

Time to skedaddle!

And yet in his heart of heart of *hearts* he knew he could not.

He was not a chicken.

Or, for that matter, a cooked goose.

Yet.

He was a superhero.

Of sorts.

And (regardless of how lame he thought his power was) he'd come to understand that with the power came responsibility.

Even if that responsibility was the decidedly distasteful duty of saving his science teacher's life.

And so, rather than turning tail and running, Dave gave a quiet command:

"Take me to the skybox."

Chapter 20
PIT OF PLUMES

Before I tell you what happened in the skybox, I really must backtrack and let you know what became of the Bandito Brothers.

You may recall that Tito was having a flapping good time in goose feathers and wanted to have a (pillowless) pillow fight with Angelo. Angelo, however, was in no mood for fun of any kind. He was furious with Pablo for kicking him off the rope (although he had tried to do the same to Pablo), and he now had fluffy feathers sticking to him all over his head, shoulders, and hands.

This was not a simple matter of static electricity holding the fine downy parts of the feathers to Angelo's hairy body.

Oh no.

This was a simple matter of being tarred and feathered. (The "tar," in this case, being the pour-on-pancakes variety that Pablo had glubbed all over Angelo.)

Angelo now looked like a big, fluffy-wuffy (and furiously clucky) bandoliered chicken.

Of course, when Pablo came plummeting into the Pit of Plumes moments later (having lost his footing and then his grip), he, too, became coated in feathers. Tickly-wickly feathers that stuck to his chest, his shoulders, and (most annoyingly of all) his face.

"Pthwwwthhh!" Pablo spat, trying to de-feather his lips. "Pthwwwthhh!" But the more he pthwwwthhhed (or swiped, or rubbed, for that matter), the worse it seemed to get.

So, in the tradition of brothers everywhere (whether of common blood or not), Pablo gave up on solving the problem and began pounding on Angelo.

Angelo (keeping with tradition) began pounding back, and Tito got into the action by squealing, "Wheeeee! Wheeeee!" and throwing feathers over them.

In no time at all, the place was an enormous fluff bowl. And, as things continued to fluffify, the Brothers sank deeper and deeper into the plumes until all at once all three seemed to realize they were in danger of dying by fluffy-wuffy suffocation.

So, just like that, the fight was over.

Just like that, the three of them swam through feathers over to the chicken-wire shore and, using the wooden cross-supports, climbed out of the Pit of Plumes.

Just like that, they got back to tracking down Dave.

"Which way do we go?" Angelo asked as they took in the rickety bridge to Goose Island, the gated tunnel that went toward daylight, the oversized foil hose sticking out of the cave wall, and the cobblestone pathway.

And although they might well have gone over the bridge or explored the foil hose, Tito discovered something that kept them on the right path. He picked up a small grassy chunk from the cobblestone pathway and murmured, "More Rosie poo-*poos*?" (placing emphasis on the second *oo* like a fancy Frenchman).

And yes, that's exactly what Tito had discovered.

Dave, you see, had been walking around with Rosie's intestinally processed weeds (and arugula) caught in the deep tread of his sneakers. And as he had sneaky-toed through the mansion, he had unwittingly dropped little stink nuggets.

Tito had spotted two of these nuggets at the rim of the Bottomless Pit (which, as we have learned, wasn't bottomless at all). And now, after a quick analysis (known, I'm afraid, as the sniff test), Tito scratched his head and wondered, What are Rosie poo-*poo*s doing here?

And then, in a sudden (and uncharacteristic) moment of clarity, he understood.

"This way!" he cried to Angelo and Pablo. "Follow the poo-*poo*s!"

"What?" the Brothers asked (each giving Tito a feather-faced squint). But as Tito disappeared up the steps, they (for once) tagged along without a fight.

And so it was that by following this trail of nuggets (or, if you prefer, poo-*poo*s), the Brothers managed to track Dave to the skybox just as Dave sneaky-toed inside.

So! Let's take inventory, shall we?

There's a devilishly demented villain wrapping duct tape around the scalpel-happy hands of a conked-out (and securely blindfolded) science teacher.

(Check, and check.)

There's a boy and his klepto-gecko hanging from the ceiling of the skybox.

(Check, and check again.)

There are three men wearing bandoliers of (useless) ammunition—two of them covered in fluffy-wuffy feathers, the other holding a collection of donkey doo.

(Check, check, and stinky-winky check!)

Which brings us to the point where the poo-*poo*s hit the fan.

"There he is!" Pablo cried, muscling his way past Angelo and Tito into the skybox.

Damien's head snapped around at the sound of Pablo's voice, his eyes burning like dark coals of anger. But as he rose to unleash his fury upon them, he saw that Pablo and Angelo were . . . tarred and feathered?

And that Tito was holding . . . donkey doo?

"Look out, boss!" Pablo cried, pointing at the ceiling above him.

But as Damien looked up, Dave let loose and did a flying twist, bombing the demented villain with a body slam that knocked him off his feet and into the open coffin.

"You fools!" the treasure hunter screeched from inside the coffin. And although his voice was muffled, it still carried such venomous anger that (for a moment) the Brothers recoiled.

Dave, however, was on adrenaline overload and couldn't let a little thing like a venomous voice from inside a coffin stop him. He shoved Damien's flailing legs into the coffin, slammed down the lid, and fastened one of the latches. Pablo was almost upon him now, so, lickety-split, Dave escaped by zippy-toeing up the wall and across the ceiling, dropping down beside Ms. Veronica Krockle (who was slumped in the chair with a roll of duct tape dangling from her wrists).

"*Asombrrrrroso!*" Sticky said. "You are getting the hang of being a gecko!"

Then, as he watched the Bandito Brothers, he whispered, "So, *señor*. What now?"

What now, indeed! It was three men (and a screaming coffined villain) against one boy (and a lizard). And in order to get Veronica Krockle out of the skybox, Dave and Sticky had to wheel her past the Brothers (who were smack-dab in the way).

It appeared that they were trapped.

Outsized and outnumbered.

In a word, toast.

But something very strange was happening.

Or, more accurately, *not* happening.

Rather than pouncing on Dave, all three Brothers simply stared at him. (Well, Tito was staring at Sticky, waving and pulling silly faces, but the point is, none of them were pouncing as one might expect.)

Then Angelo said, "He's bewitched, I tell you. Or he's not of this earth." His voice was raspy. His knees were rubbery. The hairs all over his tarred and feathered body were shaking in their roots.

"Let me out! Let me out!" Damien screeched from inside the coffin.

But Pablo (who was standing right beside the latched latch) didn't budge. He, too, just stared at Dave, petrified by what he'd witnessed. "I believe you now," he said to Angelo, his teeth chattering. "He has no suction cups."

"Let me out, you fools, so I can kill you!"

"*Señor*," Sticky whispered ever so quietly in Dave's ear. "Yell something. Make your voice low and horrible, then charge!"

"But you told me never to speak around them!" Dave whispered through his bandanna.

"That's the madman, not them!" Sticky whispered. "He's the one who remembers voices!" But after a moment, he added, "Okay, *señor*, I'll do it." He paused. "Ready?"

"You bungling bozos! LET ME OUT!"

"Ready," Dave whispered.

And with that, Sticky blasted the room with a deep, growling . . .

"MOVE!"

The Bandito Brothers hit the walls like they'd been swept aside by shock waves, and (although his ear was now ringing with pain) Dave wasted no time. He engaged the tricked-out tires of Damien's chair and wheeled Ms. Veronica Krockle out the door and down the pathway toward Goose Island.

Chapter 21
TRAPPED ON GOOSE ISLAND

Dave had not been thinking past the skybox door. His focus had been wholly and solely on getting himself (and the conked-out Ms. Krockle) around the Bandito Brothers and away from Damien Black. So, as he barreled along the cobblestone pathway, he was, at first, simply relieved.

He was moving!

Fast!

And the chair was amazing!

It was taking the bumps and dips and twists and turns like an ATV!

He even hitched himself on during the straightaways and *flew*.

Poor Dave. He wasn't thinking about the five

steep steps at the end of the pathway. Or that the chair had no brakes. (Or parachutes or air bags or bumper guards, for that matter.) He wasn't thinking that if the chair broke, he'd have no way to wheel Ms. Krockle out of there. That he'd have to *carry* her. Or that she almost certainly weighed more than he did, and that carrying her would require more than Gecko Power—it would require Super Strength. (Which was, in fact, a potential power, but not an ingot he happened to possess.)

No, Dave just blithely barreled along until Sticky whispered, "I think she's waking up!" in Dave's ear.

Dave now noticed that although his science teacher was still slumped over, her hands seemed to be moving and her blindfold seemed to have slipped. Dave thought this might be the result of all the thumping and bumping they were doing and said, "Check, would you?" as he steered through a sharp turn.

So, lickety-split, Sticky zippy-toed off Dave's shoulder and onto Ms. Veronica Krockle.

The blindfold had, indeed, slipped, but her eyes were shut.

Except, Sticky now noticed, there were slits.

Little sneaky-peeky slits.

Still. He wasn't sure.

So he zippy-toed closer, reached up, and pried an eyelid back with his sticky-toed hand.

Well! Ms. Veronica Krockle was, indeed, awake. She had simply been doing her bumpy-bouncy best to

figure out why in the world she was flying along a cobblestone walkway in a turbocharged office chair. But she now found herself eyeball to eyeball with a lizard.

A gecko lizard who seemed to be cocking an eyebrow.

A gecko lizard who seemed to be scowling at her.

A gecko lizard who snorted, then opened his mouth and grumbled, "Faker."

Ms. Veronica Krockle screamed, then immediately fainted.

Dave (distracted by the commotion with Sticky and Ms. Krockle) realized too late that straight ahead of them were steps.

"Aaaah!" he cried, pulling back on the chair.

Unfortunately, office chairs (be they turbo or standard issue) are not equipped with seat belts. So although the chair's momentum was halted at the edge, Ms. Veronica Krockle's was not.

She took off like a shot.

Catapulted like a rock.

Flew like a teacher torpedo!

And Sticky (who was still on her lab coat at liftoff) went flying, too. "Holy hurling *habañeroooooos!*" he cried, flailing through the air.

"Sticky!" Dave shouted, and as he raced to his little buddy's side, the turbo chair slipped away and landed with a clunky-crunchy crash, breaking both a leg and an arm.

Sticky, it turned out, was fine. (He'd had much worse falls before and survived them no problem.) But if a chair is going to break a leg and an arm from a tumble, you'd expect a human being to fare much worse.

In this case, however, there were geese.

And it just so happened that Ms. Veronica Krockle torpedoed straight into a gathering of geese that didn't have the chance to scatter before she landed on them.

Can you say "pâté"?

If not, never mind. The point is, she survived, and once Dave and Sticky had regrouped, they were left with a very real dilemma:

How would they ever get the conked-out Ms. Krockle over the island and through the gate before Damien showed up?

"Just wake her up!" Sticky said, then zippy-toed up to her chest and started slapping her cheeks.

"Stop!" Dave said, then got busy refastening her blindfold. "I don't want her to see me if I can help it!"

Sticky crossed his arms. "So, *señor*, how are you going to get her out of here?"

Dave looked around. "I have no idea."

Sticky gave a slow nod. "Good thinking."

"Hey! We got her this far, didn't we?" Then, miffed by Sticky's superior attitude, Dave grabbed the back collar of Ms. Krockle's lab coat and began dragging her toward Goose Island.

Sticky stayed aboard Ms. Krockle like he was riding a slow-moving surfboard. *"Ouchie-huahua,"* he said with a tisk. "That is going to hurt."

"Got a better idea, big shot?" Dave snapped over his shoulder.

Sticky didn't. And instead of continuing to surf along on Ms. Krockle and snipe at Dave, he scurried up to Dave's shoulder and mumbled, "Sorry, *señor.*"

"Look," Dave said. "I can't worry about her bumps and bruises. I've got to get her *out* of here. That madman's going to show up any minute, and when he does, it's all over."

And so Dave trudged along while Ms. Veronica Krockle thumpity-wump-bumped behind (leaving high-heeled-boot skids in her wake). Over the rickety bridge they went, across the island, over a half-drowned log, until they were (at last) at the gate.

The very tall, very locked gate.

Not that there was a padlock.

Or a handprint scanner.

Or a death laser.

It was just . . . locked.

Unopenable.

Rattle, kick, shake, and pummel proof.

And after trying everything he could think of, Dave gave the bars one final shake and said, "There's got to be a release lever somewhere!"

Then several things happened all at once:

Ms. Veronica Krockle began to groan. (And really, who could blame her?)

Sticky scurried off Dave's shoulder, calling, "I'll be right back, *señor!*" because he had noticed something odd about a nearby goose.

And finally, Damien Black entered the cave (followed in breathless pursuit by all three Bandito Brothers).

"Bwaa-ha-ha-ha-ha-ha-ha!" Damien laughed as he swooped down the steps. He hurried toward

Dave with an evil sneer. "You are trapped, boy!
You are *mine*."

Dave's heart hammered in his chest.

He looked around frantically.

He was doomed!

Chapter 22
THE GHASTLY GOOSE

While Damien was swooping toward Dave and Dave was looking around frantically for an escape, Sticky was discovering that the odd goose he'd spotted was, in fact, a fake goose. A metal one, with lopsided eyes, painted poles for legs, and sadly patchy feathers.

And it ticked.

Or, more accurately, ticktocked.

Sticky did not for an instant think that it was a bomb.

Perhaps he *should* have, but he didn't.

After all, why would Damien have a decoy bomb in the midst of his gaggle of geese?

Think of the mess it would cause if it went off.

Think of the feathers!

No, knowing Damien Black as he did, Sticky immediately suspected that this ghastly goose was some sort of diabolical doodad that did . . . *something*.

Opened a trapdoor?

Whooshed down a net?

Something.

And, given the perilous predicament they presently found themselves in, Sticky reasoned that *something* was better than nothing.

But how to make that something happen?

Sticky could find no levers, no buttons, no switches . . . just feathers!

But then he discovered a smooth crack at the base of the neck.

Not a crack . . . a joint!

Which meant that the neck moved somehow.

But how?

Sticky followed the crack around to the chest and realized that the whole, long neck was a lever (and the head was the handle).

Now, Sticky is one speedy gecko, and all this zipping around the ghastly goose had taken him only about ten seconds. Unfortunately, that was enough time for Damien and the Bandito Brothers to make it halfway across the island.

Sticky knew there was no time to lose. He took a deep breath, then turbo-toed up the ghastly goose neck, and with a mighty flying kick, he slammed down on the goose head, then flipped around, slid down the face, and held on to the beak, pulling the creaky neck lever down . . . down . . . down.

Immediately there was a noise.

A whirring, sucking, high-winds noise.

Immediately the large foil hose shot out from the cave wall and began whipping back and forth like an enormous elephant trunk.

Immediately Damien Black reacted in a way he had never (I promise you *ever*) reacted before.

He screamed.

He danced about, dodging the hose.

He screamed again.

Yes, the calculating, conniving, coldhearted Damien Black did what diabolically devilish men rarely do.

He totally lost it.

Sticky, you see, had overridden the automatic timer on the Komodo dragon's feeding hose. A feeding hose that sucked geese into the dragon pit during periods when Damien was, say, traveling.

Or incarcerated.

Or just too lazy to feed the oversized reptile himself.

And now Damien was nose to hose with a vacuum so strong that it could whisk him through a hundred feet of tubing and drop him with a painful plop into a man-eating dragon's sand pit.

He was, to put it mildly, in deep, diabolical
doo-*doo*s.

"What is that, boss?" Pablo yelled over the
whirring, sucking, high-winds noise.

But before Damien could shout, "Dive in and
find out, you fool!" the tube swung straight for

him and, with a WHOOSH, SLURRRRRP, "AAAAAAAAAAHHHHHHHH," swallowed him up.

Ah, poor Damien.

Foiled by his own foil tube.

Now, while all this screaming and whooshing was going on, Ms. Veronica Krockle had staggered to her feet, crying, "Darling!" But blindfolded and bound with duct tape, she stumbled about, fell against the gate, and hit her head.

Conked out again.

And although the ghastly goose neck had creaked its way to an upright position (and Sticky had skedaddled back to Dave), one cock of the lever activated the tube for a full two minutes. It flailed back and forth, slurping up one goose, then another while the Bandito Brothers (very wisely) backed away.

Then Pablo looked over at Dave and saw him moving his arms from side to side as though he were conducting the hose. "HE'S A DEMON!" Pablo screamed, and the three Brothers ran back to the cobblestone pathway as fast as they could.

"*Genio* beanio!" Sticky cried when the Brothers were gone and the hose had retracted. He slapped five on Dave. "That was *asombroso, señor!*"

"You're the one who saved us, Sticky! How did you know about that fake goose? And what *is* that hose thing?"

Sticky's little eyes got big. "*Ay caramba.* I'm afraid to think about it, *señor*. Did you hear the way that evil *hombre* screamed?"

Dave shivered, then looked around. "Let's get out of here, huh?"

But the question remained: How?

And even if they could break out, how would they ever get Ms. Veronica Krockle down from Raven Ridge? Dave couldn't see balancing her on his handlebars. And dragging her that far was out of the question (no matter how much he disliked her).

So how?

The answer came in the form of a butterfly.

A cheerful little yellow butterfly that flittered and fluttered through the bars of the gate and into the goose cave.

And no, little yellow butterflies (or butterflies of any kind) cannot transport thirteen-year-old boys and their conked-out science teachers out of a cave, down a mountain, and into the city. (This is, after all, a *true* story.)

But what followed the little yellow butterfly was something that *could* help them.

"Rosie!" Sticky called through the gate, and although he and the bucktoothed donkey had a history together, Rosie did not, in fact, understand a word Sticky was saying.

She did, however, recognize his voice.

And she did move closer.

And as Dave reached out to grab her (thinking who knows what), he stepped on the bottom brace of the gate (just like your mother always told you *not* to), which (ironically enough) activated the gate's release mechanism.

"*Ay caramba!*" Sticky cried as the gate swung open. "We are free!"

And, indeed, they were.

Chapter 23
WHAT YOU DON'T KNOW

Getting Ms. Veronica Krockle away from Damien's property was no small feat.

And Dave's Gecko Power was of no help whatsoever.

The duct tape, however, was. And after draping the (still-unconscious) science teacher over Rosie's back and securing her with rounds of tape, Dave and Sticky made it through the frightening forest (without interference from even one bwaa-ha-cawing raven), retrieved his bike, and led Rosie and (the snoring) Ms. Krockle to a house about a mile down Raven Ridge. There, they (very carefully) laid Ms. Krockle on the porch (with duct tape and blindfold removed), set Rosie

free (with a sharp "Arrrrreee!" from Sticky), and did a classic ding-dong ditch.

After they saw (from their spy spot) that a lady answered the door and called, "Harold, come quick! A woman's collapsed on our porch!" they continued down to the city on Dave's bike.

"They'll get her to a doctor," Dave said into the wind.

"*Sí, señor,*" Sticky called from inside the Roadrunner Express sweatshirt Dave had switched into.

"She'll tell the police!" Dave called.

"*Sí, señor!*"

"Damien will get arrested!"

"*Sí, señor!*" Sticky called, then muttered, "Unless he's already dead."

"What was that?" Dave called.

"Never mind, *señor!*"

And so Dave tore into town and did his deliveries (two of which wound up late, but forgivably so), raced home, and fell into his regular routine of spatting with his sister, doing his homework, and dragging through his chores.

But he was alive, right?

And he'd saved Ms. Krockle, right?

And all's well that ends well, right?

And since I have, admittedly, gone on rather long already, now would be a good place to stop.

Right?

Hmm. But if I stopped right now, you would never know that Ms. Veronica Krockle did *not* report what had happened to the police.

Or that Damien Black *did* survive.

Or that there was another strange science substitute at school the next day.

Or that Lily approached Dave at school and whispered, "So where were you during drama yesterday, delivery boy?"

No, you'd know none of that.

You also wouldn't know that it was because of

the Bandito Brothers that Damien's life was spared. They had (in a bumbling, you're-so-stupid-no-you're-so-stupid sort of way) managed to rescue Damien by using controls in the skybox to lower a craned net into the dragon pit.

Damien, of course, acted furious once he was safe, shouting, "You bumbling blockheads! You nettling numskulls! You idiotic idiots! You miserable morons! You dim-witted dunces! You . . . you feather-faced freaks!" as he stormed back into the house.

What upset him so much wasn't just that he'd almost been killed by his precious dragon, or that his prisoner had escaped, or that he'd spent three agonizing days as a substitute at the wrong school, or that the boy had (once again) gotten away . . . it was also the Brothers. He wanted so badly to be rid of them, but (as if things weren't bad enough already) they were now reminding him at every turn how they had saved his life.

Ah, poor Damien. He fretted, he brooded, he pouted, he stewed.

How had things come to this?

Was he losing his touch?

His grip?

His stranglehold on all things evil?

So they saved him, so what! They were fools! Why couldn't he just toss them to the dragon and be done with it?

It was, indeed, a dark and dismal day for Damien Black. But it could have been much worse had Veronica Krockle told the police her story. Oh, she babbled on about a dashing man and a magnificent dragon, but no one could make sense of what she was saying. In the end, she was hospitalized and evaluated for psychiatric care, but even she wasn't certain the whole matter hadn't been but a dream.

Except for the fact that there were four painful bumps on her head.

And her backside was all battered and bruised.

Plus her lab coat was destroyed, and her boots were ruined.

So she knew it was not, in fact, a dream, but it still felt like it. And when she was at last released to her own care, she took a leave of absence from teaching and vowed that someday, someway, she would be reunited with her dashing man and his magnificent dragon.

She was, after all, in love, and love has power stronger than anything.

(Even stronger, perhaps, than a magic Aztec wristband.)

So you see? If I had ended earlier, you would know none of that.

You would also not know that Damien Black is already back at his dastardly drawing board masterminding a new, doubly diabolical plan (with grisly gadgets to match). And oh, what a doozy of a plan it is! Not only is he plotting to—

Ah, but I really must stop now.

I am, after all, way over time.

For now, Dave is safe.

Sticky is happy.

The wristband is in the hands of good, not evil.

And so, my friend, for today, the time has come to say . . .

Adiós!

A GUIDE TO SPANISH AND STICKYNESE TERMS

adiós (Spanish / *ah-DEE-ohs*): goodbye, see ya later, alligator

ándale (Spanish / *AHN-duh-lay*): hurry up! come on! get a move on!

asombroso (Spanish / *ah-sohm-BRO-so*): awesome, amazing

ay-ay-ay (Spanish and a Sticky favorite): depending on the inflection, this could mean oh brother, oh please, or you have *got* to be kidding!

ay caramba (Spanish and a Sticky favorite / *ai cah-RAHM-bah*): oh wow! or oh brother! or I am not believing this!

bobo (Spanish / *BO-bo*): dumb, foolish, silly

bobos banditos (Stickynese / *BO-bohs bahn-DEE-tohs*): crazy bandits, stupid thieves

casa (Spanish / *CAH-suh*): house

easy-sneezy (Stickynese): piece of cake, no sweat

freaky *frijoles* (Stickynese / *free-HO-lays*): literally, weird beans. But for Sticky, oh wow! or how strange!

gaucho (Spanish / *GOW-cho*): herdsman, cowboy

genio beanio (Stickynese / *HEH-nee-oh*): genius! brilliant!

híjole (Spanish / *EE-ho-lay*): wow!

hombre (Spanish / *AHM-bray*): man, dude

hopping/hurling *habañeros* (Stickynese / *ah-bahn-YAIR-ohs*): literally, hopping hot peppers. But for Sticky, oh my gosh!

horroroso (Spanish / *hor-ur-OH-so*): horrible, terrifying, awful

lobo (Spanish / *LO-bo*): wolf

loco (Spanish / *LO-co*): crazy, loony

loco-berry burritos (Stickynese): literally, crazy-berry rolled tortilla sandwiches. But for Sticky, extra-specially crazy

mi'jo (Spanish / *MEE-ho*): dear, darling, my son, my love. For a girl, you'd say *mi'ja* (*MEE-ha*)

plumas (Spanish / *PLOO-mahs*): feathers

señor (Spanish / *SEN-yohr*): mister

señorita (Spanish / *sen-yohr-EE-tah*): miss, young lady

sí (Spanish / *see*): yes